CURRY MANGO. DAHL AND ROTI

A Novel by

Ashley Prendergast

Published by O. Mitchell Books

First edition, 2025

Published by O. Mitchell Books
ISBN: 979-8-218-79000-4
Cover design by Karter, Jasmine, and Raya
Printed in the United States of America

For more information, visit: Omitchellbooks.net or follow us on Instagram @PrenwiththePen

To my first cousins Andre, Tiffany, Catherine, Andrew, Shanice, Kevin, Candy, Skyla, and Shania, and to my sister Alexis—this book is for you.

Though we are now scattered across the world, living lives far away from where we began, you are still my foundation. My first love. The ones who taught me the meaning of loyalty, laughter, and belonging. From Harbour View to Vineyard town, we filled our days with joy—crowding together in that big house, lapping up during movie nights like we couldn't get close enough. Van-back rides to the country, sticky with bag juice and sunshine. Games of stuck and pull, dandy shandy in the yard. We were always supposed to be help fold clothes—that rocking chair would be piled high—but somehow, we always found a way to avoid it.

And at the end of every adventure, the safety of Mama and Papa's arms was always waiting.

I would give anything to relive those moments—to hear our childhood echo through those halls one more time.

This book is for you.

For everything we were

For everything you still are to me.

To Uncle Dully,

There are some debts that can never be repaid. What you did for my grandparents—no words will ever be enough.

You were the bridge that kept their love alive. The quiet messenger delivering handwritten dreams between two people who would one day build the life that led to mine. You were my grandfather's right hand, his trusted wingman, his closest companion. Through every chapter—good, bad, and heartbreaking—you stood by him.

You were there.

And when the day came that my grandfather left this world, I know you didn't just lose a relative… You lost your best friend.

Thank you for everything, Uncle Dully. You are part of the reason we're here. Your loyalty, your quiet strength, your love—it lives on in every story I write and every breath we take.

With deepest gratitude,

Ashley

EPIGRAPH

"They came across the sea, men and women from a land of ancient customs, their wrists still warm with the weight of gold bangles and promise. Brought to a strange island not by choice, but by hope and survival, they worked the soil with tired hands and carried their traditions like heirlooms in their hearts.

In this new land, they planted roots that stretched deep into cane fields, into community, into custom. Arranged marriage was not just a norm, it was protection, alliance, legacy.

But with time came change. Children born of island sun and Indian blood began to dream of choosing love over arrangement, voice over silence. And that choice, beautiful, bold, rebellious, would not come without cost.

This is the story of those who honored tradition, those who broke from it, and the women caught between duty and desire, where love is not only felt but fought for."

PREFACE

The inspiration for this novel was born in the quiet, aching days after my grandmother passed away. I had spent hours writing her eulogy, pouring memories, emotion, and gratitude into words, and when I finished, my cousin looked at me and said, “You should write a book.” I carried that idea in my heart for years, scribbling pieces of stories, starting manuscripts I couldn’t finish, losing and rediscovering my voice. But when I finally sat down with purpose, I wrote until I couldn’t stop. And this book, this story, came to life.

As a child, one of my deepest comforts was a meal prepared by my grandmother, affectionately known as Mama, Aunt Dar, or Second Mother. She had a warmth that made you feel safe just by being near her. Her curry mango, dahl, and roti was not just food, it was legacy. Before she died, Mama made sure to teach us her specialty dishes. At the time, I didn’t understand the treasure she was handing down. I wrote the recipe in a notebook during college, but never made time to recreate it. It wasn’t until years later that I realized how sacred that moment truly was.

We inherit so many pieces of culture, some we preserve and others we let go. For me, this dish came to represent more than comfort. It held the weight of family bonds, identity, survival, and the sacrifices of generations before me. Our traditions, like our stories, are carried forward not just through memory, but through what we choose to honor. One day, I hope my grandchildren will think of curry mango, dahl, and roti when they need to feel close to their roots.

My grandmother was a woman of strength and grace. Though she faced hardship, especially from some of her in-laws, she responded only with kindness. Through every challenge, she remained devoted: a wife, a mother, a grandmother, an aunt, a sister, and a daughter-in-law. This story, while fictional, carries her spirit. It reflects the tension between arranged marriages and love matches, between duty and choice, and the beauty of finding your voice in a world that often asks women to be silent.

This is my love letter to her and to the legacy we carry.

Table of Contents

CHAPTER 1 BIRTH OF THE COOLIE

They came with nothing but their names, sewn into the hems of their garments, like secrets. Names that would be changed anyway. My great grandparents left India, not as husband as wife, but as strangers who would be eventually thrown together across the ocean on contracts they could barely read. The boat smelled of sweat, rot, and broken promises, but something still bloomed in their hearts. In a land that called them coolies and made their gods foreign, they found each other. And in that finding, they changed the course of our bloodlines forever.

In the heart of 1922 amidst the golden fields of sugar cane in Jamaica, 2 lives destined to intertwine begin their journey. Asha, a young Indian woman had crossed oceans from the dusty shores of her homeland seeking a better life on this island; Raj, a quiet but determined man shared a similar fate having left his village in search of new opportunities, bound by the hardships of life as indentured laborers on the plantation. They find solace in one another's company, a spark of hope in a world that offers little to those who are far from home as the sun sets over the vast expanse of the plantation, their love story begins shaped by the unspoken dreams of two souls caught between the cultures of their past and the promise of a new future.

The warm Jamaican night was alive with the sounds of laughter, music, and the soft hum of the sugar cane fields swaying under the moonlight. It was the evening of Diwali, the festival of lights, and Kingston, though far from the lands of India, seemed to glow with the spirit of celebration. The air was thick with the scent of jasmine and sweet fried treats, and the streets were filled with men and women, their faces lit by the flickering flames of oil lamps that adorned every home, shop, and temple.

Raj had never truly believed in the magic of Diwali, not in the way the elders did. Born in the dusty village of Calcutta, he had left India months ago, journeying across the ocean as an indentured servant. His hands were now calloused from working the sugar cane fields, and the customs and rituals felt distant, echoes of a life he no longer knew. Yet tonight there was something different in the air. The glow of the lamps seemed to reach deeper into his soul, and for the first time since arriving in Jamaica, Raj felt a tug at his heart, a connection to something larger than the work and struggles of his daily life.

He stood at the edge of the small gathering in the courtyard of the Indian temple, observing the men and women who had come together to celebrate. The temple had been decorated with garlands of marigolds, their bright orange petals contrasting against the dark evening sky. The gentle rhythm of a dull drum echoed in the distance, blending with the soft melodies of a sitar and the flicker of thousands of diyas. They created a mesmerizing sea of lights, and in the center of it all stood Asha.

Asha had been in Jamaica longer than Raj. Her face was partially illuminated by the soft glow of the lamps, and Raj could not help but be drawn to her. She was unlike any woman he had ever seen before. There was an undeniable grace in the way she moved, a quiet strength in her posture. Asha was arranging a tray of sweets, her delicate fingers carefully placing the ladoo and jalebi beside the clay lamp which she would light in honor of the goddess Lakshmi. Her dark hair cascaded down her back in a loose braid, and her simple but elegant red sari shimmered in the light, the fabric catching the glow of the lamps like a flame itself.

Raj had seen her many times before in passing, yet he had never approached her. Asha exuded confidence. She had been on the plantation for at least five years and knew her way through Jamaica much more than Raj. He found himself standing at a distance, unsure of how to approach such beauty. The other men, dressed in their best kurtas, surrounded the women, offering gifts and exchanging pleasantries. Raj was too shy, aware of his rough hands and worn-out shoes, the marks of labor that defined his existence. He had longed to approach her, but something had always held him back. What could a beautiful woman like Asha see in a man like him?

As if sensing his hesitation, Asha looked up from her task. Her eyes met his for a brief moment, and his heart skipped. There was no judgment in her gaze, only curiosity, perhaps even a hint of something deeper. She offered him a small, warm smile before returning to her task, but that smile, simple and fleeting, was enough to stir something deep within him.

The music whirled around them as the festival continued, yet Raj stood frozen, watching her. The energy of the night was vivacious, the spirit of Diwali very much alive in Kingston, Jamaica. Thousands of miles away from home, it felt as though they were back in their village. The holiday carried the energy of new beginnings, and that feeling seemed to pulse through the air. Raj realized this was a moment he could not let pass.

He walked closer, slowly, unsure of himself but drawn to her in a way he could not explain. As if she felt the shift, Asha looked up once more as Raj reached her. She tilted her head slightly, acknowledging his presence. The world seemed to fade away, leaving only the two of them standing in the glow of the lamps, as if the entire festival were held together by this one quiet connection.

“Good evening,” Raj said, his voice soft but steady.

Asha smiled again, her lips curling slightly, but this time the warmth in her eyes was unmistakable.

“Good evening. You’re new here, aren’t you?”

Raj nodded. “Yes, I’ve been here a few months now. Work is hard, but the people, they make it feel like home.”

Asha’s gaze softened. “It’s not home,” she said, her voice tinged with the quiet sadness of a shared experience. “But it is where we are now, and tonight we will celebrate what we still have."

Her words resonated deeply with Raj. He had left India to find a better life. Beginning in the late 1800s, thousands of Indians boarded ships bound for the Caribbean. They were promised dreams of work, money, and a better future. Asha and Raj had both embarked from India and arrived in Jamaica, but what they found was a world that felt just as far away from home as the one they had left behind. Still, tonight, Diwali had reminded them of hope, of new beginnings, of light after darkness, of the possibility of something beautiful emerging from struggle.

"Diwali," Raj said, "is a reminder to light a lamp even in the darkest places."

Asha smiled, her expression thoughtful. "Yes. It is a reminder that even in a place like this, where everything seems difficult, there is always light to be found."

She held out a sweet from the tray. "Would you like one?"

Raj hesitated for a moment before accepting the treat. As he took it from her, their fingers brushed lightly and Raj felt a jolt of electricity, a connection that went beyond touch. He looked into her eyes, and in that moment something unspoken passed between them: an understanding, a recognition of shared experience.

“Thank you,” he said softly. The sweetness of the ladoo faded into the background as his mind remained fixed on the beauty in front of him.

Asha nodded, a knowing smile playing at the corner of her lips. She stepped back slightly, returning to her task, but Raj stayed where he was, watching her. There was something magnetic about her, something that made him feel, for the first time since arriving in Jamaica, that perhaps this place could be more than just a stopover in his life.

As the night wore on, the crowd grew louder, but Raj and Asha remained in their quiet world, exchanging fleeting glances and words that lingered just long enough to stir a spark. Amidst the celebrations, as firecrackers exploded in the sky, Raj realized that his journey had brought him here, to this moment. A simple touch, a smile, and the warmth of a shared celebration lit a flame in his heart. It was the beginning of something he had not expected, something beautiful and uncertain. Yet in the glow of a diya, Raj knew one thing for sure. This was just the beginning.

The night of Diwali passed in a blur of lights, music, and fleeting conversations. But for Raj, everything seemed to slow when he was near Asha. As the festivities continued into the late evening, the sounds of fireworks and laughter filled the air, but Raj found himself lost in the quiet warmth that Asha carried with her.

The next morning, after the last firecracker had faded and the glowing diya had been extinguished, Raj walked through the sugar cane plantation as the sun began to rise over the Kingston skyline. The city was slowly coming to life, with the smell of freshly baked bread wafting through the air and the sound of birds greeting the new day as workers gathered to tend the fields.

Raj spotted Asha in the distance, her silhouette framed by the soft light of early morning. She was walking toward a nearby stream, carrying a basket of freshly picked fruit, her sari flowing gently behind her as she moved. Raj hesitated for a moment, unsure if it was too early or inappropriate to approach her, but his feet seemed to move on their own. He followed at a distance until, as she reached the water's edge, he finally caught up to her.

"Asha," he said, his voice a little rough from the early hour, "you're awake early."

She turned, her face lighting up with recognition. “Raj,” she greeted, her voice soft and welcoming. “The morning is the only time of day when I can find some peace before my work begins.”

“I understand,” Raj said, taking in the peacefulness of the scene around them. The soft murmur of the stream was the only sound besides the rustling of the trees. The air was cool, and the scent of fresh earth mixed with the fragrance of blooming wildflowers surrounded the pair as they stood in companionable silence for a moment, each lost in the simple beauty of the morning.

“I didn’t think I’d find you here,” Raj continued. His voice was lower now, as if speaking words that had been sitting in his chest for days.

“You always seem so busy with everything—the work, the temple, your family, the preparations, the festival.”

Asha smiled, her eyes soft with the understanding of shared concerns. “The festival is supposed to be a distraction. Was it not a chance for us to forget, even for a moment, about the hard days ahead? A chance for us to live in the current moment? A chance for us to remember home, even many miles apart? But now, as we wake up, the work is still here.

The sugar must be harvested, the fields need tending. We have no choice but to rise early and face it."

Her words mirrored his own thoughts. For months Raj had labored tirelessly in the fields under the scorching Jamaican sun. His hands were blistered and raw from the endless cutting and harvesting. It was exhausting, but it was what they had to do to survive. Raj had a family—a mother, a father, little siblings back home in India—depending on him to make something of his life. Yet something about Asha's words, about her quiet acceptance, made the burden feel a little lighter.

"I'm glad you are here," Raj said, his voice softer now. "I don't think I've met anyone else who understands how hard it is, how lonely it can be sometimes."

Asha met his gaze, her expression open and unguarded. "I think we're all lonely here in our own ways," she said. "We came from different places, different lives, but we're all here together, trying to find something in this foreign land."

"For me, Diwali brought a glimpse of home. But the rest of the year in Jamaica, it's like we're waiting for something we cannot reach."

He took a step closer, his heart beating faster. There was something about Asha that drew him in: a calm, quiet strength and understanding that ran deeper than words. It was as though for the first time he was speaking with someone who could truly see him, not just the laborer or the immigrant, but the man beneath the surface.

For the next few weeks, Raj and Asha spent more time together in the mornings. They often met by the stream, sitting together in silence or talking about their lives before they had arrived in Jamaica. Asha shared stories of her childhood in a small village near Delhi. During one of the festivals, she recalled the sound of her family's laughter. She spoke of her mother, who had always told her to find joy even in the hardest of times, and her father, who had tried to shield her from the pain of their forced migration.

Raj, in turn, shared stories of his home in the wild fields of Calcutta, where his family had worked as farmers before they were promised a better life in Jamaica. He spoke of his family's hope for him, the sacrifices they had made, and the harsh realities he had faced after arriving on the island: the long days of grueling labor, the feeling of being far from home, the quiet moments of homesickness that gnawed at him. Though their stories were different, they both shared the same ache—the longing for something familiar in a place that was anything but.

One afternoon, after a long day's work, Raj and Asha walked through the bustling streets of Kingston. The market was vibrant with color: vendors selling spices, textiles, and trinkets from India, Africa, and the Caribbean. The chatter of the crowd was a mix of languages—Hindi, English, and patois. The air was thick with the aroma of jerk and curry as they strolled side by side.

Raj found himself noticing the way Asha's eyes sparkled when she saw a stall filled with bright bangles. She paused, running her fingers over the delicate glass and metal, her smile as bright as the colors around them. Without thinking, Raj reached out and picked a set of gold bangles from the table, holding them out to her.

"Try these on," he said, his voice quiet, almost shy.

Asha's eyes softened, and a blush began to form on her cheeks. "Raj, you don't have to—"

"I want to," he interrupted gently. "They're beautiful, just like you."

For a moment they both stood still, the words hanging between them like a delicate thread. Asha's heart fluttered in her chest and she felt a warmth spread through her, one that had nothing to do with the Jamaican sun.

"Thank you," she whispered. A genuine, unguarded smile took over her face, and for the first time in his life Raj felt that perhaps, amid all the hardship, something beautiful was beginning to take root.

As they continued their walk, hand in hand, the bond between them deepened. It was a connection built not just on shared experiences, but on the quiet understanding that even in the most difficult of circumstances they had something worth holding on to. And under the warm Jamaican sun, amidst the bustling market and the rhythm of the island, Raj and Asha knew that their journey together was only just beginning.

As the year turned to 1923, Raj and Asha's connection evolved. What had begun with small exchanges and stolen moments in the quiet corners of Kingston's bustling streets slowly grew into something undeniable. Their growing affection was a delicate thing. Over time, their friendship was nourished by shared values, long walks along Kingston Harbor, and conversations filled with dreams of education, community service, and preserving their heritage in a land far away from their ancestral home.

The next few weeks in the fields were especially tiring for Raj. He yearned for Asha in a way he had never known before. He could see her from two rows over, her thin frame bending with the wind, her hands moving fast but careful, as though she had something worth saving.

The overseers did not like men and women speaking too long, did not like eyes lingering or laughter between the rows. But it happened anyway. Between buckets of cut cane, glances turned to words, and words to quiet offerings—a guava left by her bedding, a copper coin tied into his kerchief.

Marriage had never been part of Raj's plan. He was here to work and return to his family. But one day, his mind shifted. It was the way she stood in the rain, barefoot in the mud, cradling a stray kitten in the folds of her skirt as if it were something sacred. The sky cracked open above them, but she did not flinch. Her eyes, dark, tired, unbroken, met his through the downpour, and in that moment Raj felt something shift in his chest. Not lust. Not even love as he had known it from stories whispered in his village. But certainty. The kind that digs its roots deep.

She had come across oceans, carried sorrow in her bones, and still found tenderness to offer a trembling thing with no name. He wanted that softness near him. He wanted her laughter in his house, her footsteps beside his, her name bound to his in a world that tried to erase them both. That was the moment. Simple. Wet. Undeniable.

The only issue was that Raj had no parents here. No village aunties or uncles to speak on his behalf. No priests to chant the mantras beneath mango trees.

One evening, after their routine harbor walk, Raj walked Asha home. He marched right up to her barrack and stood tall before her family—her mother, father, and sisters.

"I don't have gold," he said, his voice steady. "But I have hands that work, and a heart that's already hers."

There was silence, then the low murmur of approval. Her father nodded. "Then marry before the rain comes," he said. "Let the god see it and the land bless it."

By June, with the blessings of her family and the quiet approval of the local Hindu elders, they announced their engagement.

The engagement party was held in the courtyard of Asha's family home, close to the edge of town. The night was warm and star-filled, and the air was thick with the scents of ghee-laced curries, marigold garlands, and fresh mango chutney.

Women in bright saris sang traditional Bhojpuri folk songs while men smoked clove-laced cigarettes and exchanged stories of the old country. A tabla player kept rhythm as children danced barefoot under the lanterns strung between tamarind trees. There was laughter, music, and the unmistakable thrill of something beautiful and enduring taking shape.

A few short weeks later, the wedding was held.

They wed on a Sunday. A white sheet was strung up between two cane poles, and her sari was tied with threads of marigold and turmeric. Someone played a dhol drum, soft and off beat, while the men shared bottles of rum, as old as their contracts. It was a grand affair by any standard for that time period. Money was not plentiful, but the riches were found in their strength of community and family.

The mandap was set up in a garden close to the sugar cane fields. The pillars were wrapped in banana leaves and marigolds. A pundit came in from Spanish Town to conduct the ceremony in Sanskrit, and the seven pheras were walked under the watchful eyes of relatives and friends.

Asha wore a deep red sari with gold embroidery, a family heirloom that had survived the passage from India six years prior. Raj, dressed in a cream sherwani and turban, could not take his eyes off her. As the fire crackled between them and the conch shells sounded, the two became one under the Jamaican sun, before the fields called them back again.

They were bound not just by tradition and ritual, but by a love nurtured across oceans, through resilience, and within the vibrant tapestry of Jamaica's diverse soul.

The wedding feast lasted well into the night. There was roti, curry mango, dahl, curried goat, mango lassi, and sweet jalebi spun fresh on iron skillets over coal fire. Kingston pulsed with music that night, and the stars above bore witness to the beginning of a story that would span generations: one that defied geography, thrived in community, and laid down roots in the rich, hybrid soil of their new island home.

In the months after the wedding, Raj felt a sense of completeness he had never known before. Though far from the land of his ancestors, he had made a home in Jamaica filled with love, tradition, and the quiet hum of a life just beginning. Still, a promise from his youth lingered in the back of his mind: to return to India one day, to touch the soil of his birthplace, and to bring offerings to the temple where his mother had once prayed for his safe journey to the West Indies.

That promise weighed heavy on his mind. The wedding had come and gone, stitched together with joy and whispered blessings. There were no children yet, just quiet evenings filled with shared chapati and slow conversations under the almond tree. But their hearts, even joined, still beat toward home. India lived in their silences: in the way Asha traced her bangles before bed, in the way Raj saved every coin in a tin marked *Calcutta.* They spoke often of going back—how they would build a small house near his parents' village, how he would find work in the rice fields, how they would raise children who knew both the Ganges and the Caribbean Sea. But ships did not sail for sentiment, and the cost of return was measured in more than rupees. For now, they waited. Married, bound, and quietly yearning east.

They counted the years carefully. It was 1926, and Raj began making arrangements for the long-awaited return voyage. He scratched marks into the back wall of the barrack—one for each full moon, each harvest, each brutal dry season that cracked the land and their fingers alike. Asha kept their immigration papers tucked into a rusted tin under the bedding, unfolding them on Sundays like sacred scripture.

“Five years,” the papers promised in brittle ink. Five years of labor in exchange for passage back to Hindustan. Raj had carefully saved from his modest salary. In those early days he had come under an indentureship contract, his labor exchanged for passage, food, and the distant promise of land or return. He had long since fulfilled his terms but had been told he was entitled to a small gratuity and return fare. He clung to that hope as a path to close the circle of his journey, now with his new wife.

Asha, ever supportive though reluctant to part, helped him prepare. The couple spoke of returning together once they had secured a home in India. Letters were drafted, trunks packed, and farewells quietly spoken to neighbors.

At the shipping office near the harbor, Raj presented his paperwork—a thick sheaf of documents signed and countersigned by overseers, clerks, and notaries. He expected, perhaps naively, that his return passage would be honored.

But when he met with the plantation agent, the truth came down like monsoon rain on dry earth.

“We’ve completed our five years. We want to arrange passage back to India. It says here…” He carefully unfolded the worn contract. "…we are entitled to return at the end of service."

"There's been a discrepancy," the man said gruffly, flipping through the paperwork with an air of practiced indifference. "You were advanced food and supplies during your indenture, more than your due. The cost has been deducted. This contract is not valid anymore. It was revised three years ago. You coolies signed the updated one three years back."

"No," Raj said, his voice shaking but firm. "I never signed another paper."

"You stayed past the third year," the man said. "You worked. That counts as acceptance. You people don't need to sign with ink—you sign with your silence."

"We worked because we were told our contract was for five years. It was the only promise we had."

The man leaned forward, elbows on the desk. "Promise?" He laughed then, a dry, cutting sound. "You think anyone promised you anything? You're property, boy. Cane cutters. Field rats. Be glad you have a roof over your head. You coolies come here and think you're owed something."

Raj opened his mouth to speak, to protest, but no sound came. The blood rushed to his ears, and all he could hear was the word *Jamaican*—as if it were a sentence instead of a place. He had not signed anything nor been told of a revision. Somewhere between the cane and the cutting, the promise had vanished.

“I am not your property,” Raj said.

The man stood. “Well, you’re not going anywhere. You’ve no funds. No passage. And no government’s paying for you to go back to wherever you and the other coolies came from.”

He tossed the paper back at Raj like trash. “This is your home now. Make peace with it.”

Raj stood stunned. The contract he had signed at the age of nineteen—barely understanding the language—had been manipulated, twisted by those who never meant to honor its terms. He had no legal recourse; the colonial system saw men like him as labor, not claimants. The meager sum he had left would not buy him a third-class berth back to Calcutta, let alone allow travel inland to his ancestral village.

When he returned home that evening with no tickets, Asha read the truth in his face before he said a word. She held his hand tightly, pulled him inside, and whispered, “Then we stay.”

In that moment, Raj's heartbreak gave way to clarity. India would always live in his prayers, in the Sanskrit verses he taught in the evenings, in the spiced lentils Asha cooked, and in the names they would give their future children. But Jamaica—its sunlight, its struggle, its soil—was now home. His roots had stretched across the sea, and where they landed, they would grow.

By the close of 1927, Raj and Asha had settled into a small, sturdy two-room house in the middle of Franklin Town, just east of downtown Kingston. The modest home, painted in faded lime and sky blue, sat on a narrow plot shaded by breadfruit trees. In the backyard, Asha tended a thriving kitchen garden of okra, bhaji, and scallions, while Raj carved out a quiet space for prayer and reflection: an altar with images of Lakshmi, Saraswati, and Lord Rama, where incense curled into the air each morning.

That year, after days of labor and under the careful watch of a midwife from the Indian community, Asha gave birth to their first child—a girl, with thick black hair and eyes that mirrored the Caribbean Sea at dawn.

They named her Riya, meaning "happy," for her arrival had filled their lives with a happiness neither had imagined possible in the early days of their journey. Word of the birth spread quickly. Relatives and neighbors arrived with gifts: homemade sweets, soft cloths, and brass bangles. A pundit performed a small namkaran ceremony in their home. Coconut oil was rubbed into the baby's hair, prayers were whispered into her ears, and her name was written in rice on a silver tray. The women sang lullabies in Bhojpuri, their voices rising and falling like waves, while the men offered blessings and smoked hand-rolled cigarettes on the veranda.

Life moved steadily forward. Raj began working as a carpenter. He also tutored in the neighborhood, offering lessons in Hindi and mathematics by kerosene lamp. Asha, meanwhile, became the quiet backbone of their home—managing the household, helping other young mothers, and keeping the rhythms of their faith alive.

Between 1926 and 1937, the small Singh home in Franklin Town transformed into a vibrant, ever changing world of laughter, learning, and constant motion. Asha and Raj, once newlyweds in a foreign land, became the proud parents of five children, each one a symbol of resilience, faith, and the evolving Indo-Jamaican story.

Their second child, another girl, Kamla, arrived in the middle of heavy rain season during 1927, as if the skies themselves had blessed her birth. Her laughter came early, and her spirit was fierce.

Then came their first boy, Raj Jr., a strong and silent type.

Then came Alexander in 1933, a curious child with an even more curious spirit, born during the summer of unrest and rising labor protests in Kingston.

Then the last girl, Shanti, with a spirit hot like the fireside.

And lastly, in 1937, they welcomed another boy, Anil, quiet and meek, and always running behind his other siblings.

With each birth, the household reshaped itself; more cots were tucked into corners, more mouths needed feeding, more stories were told at bedtime. The older children helped with the younger ones, and Asha ran the household like a ship's captain. Mornings began with a frenzy of bathing, grooming, feeding, and dressing for the schoolhouse. Raj, still tutoring after work, kept discipline with a stern voice and steady eyes. He insisted on education for all his children, daughters and sons alike, and drilled them in arithmetic, Sanskrit prayers, and the writings of Gandhi and Tagore.

With so many children, their home swelled with life. Mornings began with the ringing of a brass bell at the altar, followed by a warm breakfast of paratha or boiled green bananas with saltfish. Afternoons brought the sound of Asha humming bhajans as she folded clothes, while Raj read from the Ramayana under the shade of the almond tree outside. In the evenings, the big family gathered on woven mats, telling the stories of Ram, Sita, and Hanuman by lantern light, their voices mingling with the sounds of crickets and distant drumming from the neighboring Afro Caribbean yards.

Despite the challenges of raising a large family in a colonial society that offered little to immigrants of Indian descent, Raj and Asha carved out a rich and meaningful life. Their yard was often full of children playing cricket with broomsticks, the sound of conch shells from nearby Rastafarian camps mixing with the chanting from their home shrine.

Their home became a gathering place, not only for Hindus but for neighbors of all backgrounds. On holidays, Asha would cook massive pots of dhal, rice, goat, mango, and roti, offering food to anyone who arrived with a blessing or a story to share. On Diwali, the entire neighborhood glowed with oil lamps, and on Emancipation Day they joined the wider Jamaican community in celebration, teaching their children both their Indian roots and their Caribbean soil. Each child grew with a sense of dual belonging, knowing the rituals of puja, the taste of tamarind balls, the rhythm of the tassa drum, and the strength of community that came from living between two worlds.

The children grew up speaking Hindi at home, patois in the streets, and English in school, blending cultures as effortlessly as breath. They learned to honor their ancestors with offerings and to respect their neighbors with open hearts. They celebrated Diwali with rows of mustard oil diyas and Christmas with borrowed joy, exchanging sugar cakes and sweet sorrel with friends across faiths and colors.

Raj often said to Asha, "Our children will know where they come from, not only the land but the soul of our people."

Asha, ever grounded, would smile and reply, "And they will know how to live where they are."

In quiet moments, Raj would look at Asha as their children played in the yard and say, "This is our legacy, not only the prayers we say or the temple we build, but them."

Asha, her sari dusted with flour from the roti dough and a child on her hip, would smile and answer, "Yes. We are no longer just visitors here. We are planting a forest."

Thus, their six children were raised in Franklin Town, Kingston, Jamaica. They were Jamaican by birth, Indian by heritage, and children of love that had crossed oceans and taken root in the heart of the island.

CHAPTER 2 YORK STREET

"By the time I came along- the 4th in a line of children born on this island- the dream of India had become something distant, like the scent of my mother's sandalwood oil: lingering but unreachable. I was not born in a village. I was born at 1 ¼ York Street in Frankling Town, Kingston, Jamaica under a zinc roof, in a yard filled with mango trees that leaned like they knew all of our secrets, goats, and a chicken shed to a woman who called me her moonlight

Born in the middle of the night, bright eyed and bawling.

They say middle child get forgetting. Not me. Mi too nuff fi get lost. From early, I knew how to shine. If my older brother was the quiet storm, I was the hurricane with style. My younger brother and sister still suck finger when me out a road playing cricket in the street, sometimes barefoot, bawling "Howzat!" louder than the umpire. I bang the dholak like I was born with it. Music, noise, wisdom, it all comes natural to me.

My mother said I get my mouth from her side, they were known for being feisty, and my fast hands from my

father. But the truth is, I was born with my charm. Mi could sweet talk old lady fi extra mango, and turn licks into lecture, meaning me get in trouble but me can talk me way out most times. If my older brother did study book, I study people. I watch. I listen. And then mi spin it back pon them. Ah nuh wicked me wicked, just quick.

My old lady used to buss my ears with love and licks. She would cuss when me bring home some new mischief. But after she done shout, she always prepare my favorite meals. I was her eye ball. The others would be upset that I was her favorite, but deep down it was because they knew no one could make her smile like me.

From the start, I had a gift for talking. Aunties at the temple said my tongue was dipped in honey. I could sell old coconuts as cricket balls if I tried. My father was a carpenter and ran a small shop with his cousin near Cross Roads, and I sometimes helped him out on the weekends and after school. Customers left with more than they came for, stories, extra dhal, even sometimes a date if they were pretty.

Ma used to say I was born under a wandering star. I'd fix radios, tend to the chickens, draw portraits for tourists down by the harbor, even played dholak for a chutney

band for three months until I got caught kissing the lead singer's sister behind the rum shop. School was optional in my mind, but I made sure I passed every exam. The world was too full of things to learn outside: how mangoes ripen faster in brown paper, how to read a woman's eyes before her words, how to patch a tire with nothing but heat and prayer. I hung around Rasta men in Parade, fisherman at Rae Town, Chinese shopkeepers in downtown, and Hindi men in the temple, all my teachers.

Still, I always made it home by sunset. That's when Ma would be in the kitchen, sari tucked up, tasting curry with her finger, humming bhajans under her breath. She loved me differently, I knew it. She would scold me for skipping class, or teasing my sisters, and tussling with my brothers, and then she would save the biggest roti for me.

Some nights, I would sit with her while she oiled my sisters' hair, and she would tell me about India. About mango trees that touched the sky, monsoons like God crying, and a river so holy it forgave anything. I'd listen, wide eyed, my fingers stained with ink and tamarind, dreaming of the world beyond the sea, but knowing I'd never leave her.

Our yard did full up by time I leaving school; five children, two parents, pot covers clanging, goat bawling in the lane, and radio playing old Indian songs on Sunday morning. Some people say chaos. I call it symphony. That's how we grow. Plenty noise, plenty fight, plenty love.

By the time I was ready to leave school, I had worked more jobs than my sisters had shoes. I helped build a radio tower, taught myself to fix carburetors, and even painted signs for a juicer named Big Joe. I could talk politics with the old men and dance calypso with the girls. I knew how to stitch a wound, write a love letter, and how to disappear just before trouble knocked.

I wasn't destined to be serious like my older brother, or naive like my little brother Anil. But I knew people. I knew how to make them laugh, question what they know, how to make them feel seen. In a place like Kingston, where everyone hustling and holding on, sometimes that's all you need.

Looking back now, I see that my story wasn't written in books or degrees, but in the hands I held, the lives I touched, and the nights under the mango trees, sweet

juice dripping down my chin, the air thick with spice and possibility.

And Ma? She always said I'd surprise everyone one day. Maybe I still will.

My older brother, Raj Jr., him too serious. Always reading some dusty book like he was a sixty year old professor trapped in a boy's body. Don't get me wrong, I was book smart too, but I applied it in real life, street smarts. Raj called me reckless; I called him boring. But we were still close. As much as I used to tease him, hide him glasses, switch out him school socks for mine, I loved him same way. He was the one who covered for me when I would sneak out, or help me study the night before a test, even though I should have been studying all two weeks before. Together, we make one solid human being.

I had sisters too. Riya was first. She was already married and gave us a niece and a nephew. They didn't live close by, but my niece and nephew stayed with us most of the year and attended the all age school in town. She is my favorite sister. There was not a time when she nuh spoil me, and now I get to bring her children along for my mischief.

Kamla was next in line. She could cuss eh? Like one market woman. But she had sense. She was the one who could look at you and tell if you was lying. So I avoided her eyes when I sneak mango from Miss Gloria tree next door, or when I claim say I never broke the window, even though the cricket bat still warm inna my hand.

The younger ones, Anil and Shanti, we called them the second batch. They did soft and noisy, always carrying news to Mama. But I couldn't vex with them for too long. Especially Anil. He used to follow me around like puppy. Everything mi do, him want do. One night him even sneak out with me and mi friend to play drum at a wedding. Mama nearly faint when she hear he was out after dark. I wasn't perfect. When my little brother Anil would stand in the mirror for hours to perfect his hair, I would walk by and toss it around, starting a tantrum. I would tease my sisters' boyfriends and find ways to outsmart them. I would take the love notes out of my little sister's notebooks and pass them to our older brother, who would not stand for none of that.

That's how it was. I tease them, yes, but I protect them too.

In our house, love was loud. Nobody hug and kiss too much, but we show love in licks, in laughter, in calling each other nickname until it stick. That's how I got my nickname Pops. I looked exactly like my father, and although I was not the oldest boy in the family, I was the one everyone came to, whether it was fixing a chair or talking someone out of punishment.

Cricket was church for me. Not the kind with hymnbook and sandals. But the kind with barefoot blessings and zinc pans for wickets. Every Sunday, once Mama finish cook and Papa drop asleep under the breadfruit tree, mi gone. Me and my best friend Jerome, tall, skinny, fast like breeze, we run to the open lot at the back of Miss Mavis' yard with one goal in mind: dominate.

We never had proper gear. One bat we share, sometimes it crack, sometimes it fix, wrapped in electrical tape and prayer. Tennis ball long out of shape, soft like mango skin. But when mi step to crease, it was over. Whole yard know my style. My grip low, my hips loose, and my eyes sharp like Papa machete.

"Bowl it den, Raj," I shout to my brother, who only knew how to play because Mama force him to come outside. Him shuffle up like him afraid of dust, then toss the ball

with one stiff arm like him a do homework. But me? Mi meet that ball with full swing and send it flying straight past Jerome, who playing wicketkeeper, right over Miss Mavis' clothesline. Whole yard shout "SIX!"

Jerome would run and tackle me like we just win West Indies Cup. He was my partner in crime, on and off the field. Him could bowl fast, real fast, even though his arm bend like banana. We used to bet juice money on games, challenge boys from other lane. I remember one time we beat a team from Allman Town and they vex so bad, one of them chase us halfway down Windward Road with a coconut branch. My foot bun up that day, but I never drop the bat.

Those were the days I felt like royalty. Not inna big house or fancy car, but right there on York Street on the dry earth, sweaty with my friends by my side and the sun blessing my back. Cricket gave me a place to shine outside of Mama's kitchen and Papa's rules. When ball a play, we forget we poor. We forget the world call we coolie and laugh at how we smell of curry and castor oil. Out there, I was just a boy with a bat, a boundary in sight, and the whole yard watching.

After the match, me feel like a superstar. My chest high, my skin full of dust, sweat, and pride. Jerome, Raji and I walk back down the lane, dragging the bat like a trophy. People on the verandas shout, "Well done, bwoy!" One girl even wink at mi from behind her mother's curtain. I winked back of course.

But once I reach 1 ½ York Street and see my old lady standing there with hand on her hip, mi know my reign done right here so. She was not smiling. She looked like a miserable market lady.

"So is cricket alone you plan fi play in this life? Yuh nah go bat fi exam paper? Scholarship nuh grow pon tree like June plum, Pops."

I tried to charm her, flash a smile, lean in fi a chups pon her cheek. She buss mi one slap pon mi arm. Not too hard, just enough fi remind me is who run things. Then she point toward the humble house.

"Go inside and wash yuh foot before you dirty up my floor. And don't touch the pot yet. Dinner not ready."

I went inside still grinning. Jerome outside laughing til him cough. I bathe with the outside pipe, flicking water like I in a spring. Then I sat by the back steps waiting for

the first whiff of roti and dhal, knowing deep down that even with all the mouth my old lady have, she was proud of me. She just hide it like she hide the good spoon when her cousin them come over. And later, when she slide me a extra sugar roti under the table, she whispered, "Good shot today."

Cause in our house, that was love. That was blessing. That was cricket.

Part 2

Evening time in our yard was like a shift change. Noise turn to hush, pot cover give way to whisper, and Papa took his seat on the back steps with a cup of bush tea and one long sigh.

Papa was once a man who laugh loud, dance at weddings, and tell stories about India like it was just a place round the bend in Rollington Town or Vineyard Town. But as we grow, he quiet down. Not bitter, just quieter. Like the years soften him up. He still call me Pops in that deep, gruff voice, still pat my back after I wash the donkey cart or catch the goat trying to run off on the road. But lately, there has been less long talk. He started listening more, staring out toward the banana trees like they held secrets from his past.

Some say time make man gentle. I think life just wore him out a bit. Those years of working the cane field, trying to get back to India and hearing "no" each time, that sort of thing turn fire into ember. Still warm, but no longer blazing.

One thing about Papa: he loved Mama quiet, and he loved us even quieter. He never shouted. He never had to. One look, that's all it took. Never beat. When he was upset, he walked. When he was pleased, he smiled small and gave a nod. When I come home from school with a C, my old lady would fling slipper. Papa, or Ba as we called him as babies, would just say, "Do better," and somehow that sting more than the slipper.

And me? I was Mama's eyeball. Her heartbeat. Second born son. She used to press her finger to my cheek and say, "You're the one God send me when I was tired and needed to laugh." I used to puff up like a balloon when she tell me those things. The others would roll their eyes. Deep down they knew the middle spot belonged to me.

My sisters, Shanti and Kamla, were different. Dainty, proud, and full of tradition. They were always helping Mama cook, sweeping yard early, oiling hair till it shine like river stone. They talk about marriage from long time. Not the love, random match Mama and Ba had. No. They wanted proper arrangements. Respectable husbands from good families.

They used to giggle over the suitors who passed by the temple, whispering which uncle was setting up who. I used to laugh at them.

"So you really think you want a stranger fi pick out your life?"

They would just kiss their teeth and screw up them market mouth.

I never understood the arranged thing. This is not India. Why choose silence over spark? Why choose someone Mama and Ba pick? But I guess everyone is not like me. Everyone can't manage fire. Some people like calm.

An image of my parents flashed in my mind just now. I recall at night after dinner, roti soft and dhal bubbling thick, Papa would sit and oil his cuticles with castor oil, Mama would hum a slow bhajan, and I would watch the

scene like a movie I halfway belonged to. Part of me in it, part of me itching to run outside and live my own story.

One night I was heading to the back to look for my shoes when I heard them whispering. Kamla and Shanti, huddled on the veranda like two hens roosting, giggling low like they didn't want the walls to hear.

"I heard he's a mechanic now," Kamla said, voice sweet like sugar roti.

"And his uncle own a bakery in Spanish Town. That's steady work."

"Steady hands too," Shanti answer, making that coy little laugh she use when she want to act like a modest lady. "And tall. Mama say tall boys bring tall pickney."

I nearly choke pon my spit. Tall pickney? What kind of metric that?

I leaned in a little closer, hiding behind the bush like I was spying for the Queen. This girl Shanti was beaming, twirling the end of her braid, eyes dreamy like she a plan wedding sari. Kamla was nodding like the matchmaker down pon Windward Road.

"And what if him stink?" I blurted out from my hiding spot.

They jumped like them see duppy.

"Pops, you fool!" Kam screech, grabbing her slipper like a weapon. "Why are you sneaking around like a mongoose?"

I came out laughing. "So unu really want a strange man come tell unu how fi live? Suppose him nuh like curry and yuh haffi cook yam and butter every night?"

Shanti fold her lanky arms. "Not everyone want to run road and chase tail like you. Some of us want a husband who come home."

"Good luck wingie, and make sure him mouth can handle spice. Don't bring no bland mouth man inna Mama kitchen."

They both kiss them teeth and chase me off, but I know I heard laughter before I reached the steps.

Truth is, I love them same way. Even when they act so above me with this marriage thing. They are good girls. Kind, smart, sweet, but they could not see the shackles

that came with the wedding ring. An arranged wedding ring at that.

Me? I wanted freedom. Love. Maybe even trouble. But at least I would have chosen it.

Later that night, I continued my eavesdropping. Mama and Ba came to a decision. No bhajan. No spoon tapping pot. No kettle whistling. Just the shuffling of Papa's slippers and Mama's sigh as she sit with her sari wrapped tight around her shoulders.

I was half asleep in the hammock when I heard it.

"They are getting older. Kamla is nineteen this year. Shanti is close behind. It's time. We cannot wait for love like we did. That was luck. Not all girls get that chance. Especially in today's age. Marriage is like a business contract now. Wealth, power, status."

Ba did not answer. I peeked through the curtain and saw him watching the firelight flicker low in the coal stove. His hands were folded in his lap, same way he sat when he was thinking deep, like the ground outside had answers only he could hear.

"You sure?" he finally said. "Did you ask them?"

I sensed this hesitance because my oldest sister had already married and we hardly saw her. We did spend time with the children, Percy and Amara. I was their best friend. But I know deep down, Ba missed his first girl more than anything.

Mama nodded. "Kamla wants a match from temple. A nice family, food name. Shanti too. They want the structure, the order. That's how girls stay safe. Protected."

"BUT WE CAN PROTECT THEM," Ba said.

"What about my name? My legacy?"

"Pa, they will have status," Ma replied.

Papa shifted but said nothing else. He trusted her. That much I knew. When the old lady made up her mind, even silence was agreement.

I wanted to leave them alone, but I could not help myself. I stepped out, arms folded, voice calm but cheeky as ever.

"So we trading hearts now? Love go through committee?"

Ma looked up at me, startled but not angry. She shook her head, half smiling.

"You always have something to say. Always in someone business that is not yours."

"They are my business. My older sister got married and we hardly see her. She like a caretaker for her husband's family. We are just the day care. The other two, although not very bright, are still my sisters." I smirked. "They should be able to choose just like you did."

She sighed again, long like all of India and Jamaica was sitting on her chest.

"That was a different time. I was foolish. I lucky that your father was kind. But what if he wasn't? What if that gamble ruin my life? Kamla and Shanti don't want to gamble. They want something safe. Something rooted."

Ba finally spoke again, voice quiet but firm. "Let them decide. Bring the names. But no forcing."

Ma turned back to the fire, nodding slowly. "Fine. But we still hold tradition. We can bend it, but not break it."

Then she turned to me, her eyes softening the only way they ever did when she look at me.

"You, Pops, you different. You don't listen to nobody but yourself. Since the day you come out bawling like you

own the place. Mi let you be free, because I know you always stay by my side. Freedom is not always what every woman want."

And I could not argue with that look she gave me. That look that melt me down to the boy again. I was her favorite and she was my first love. The woman who taught me how to walk, how to drum, how to sweet talk. But even love like that comes with chains sometimes. Silken ones, yes, but chains all the same.

The next week came a pleasant morning. This was the morning of my last day of school. I woke up late on accident. I was up all night writing down a plan for a shelf I was building for Ma for the front room. Sun was already high by the time I rose, the rooster up long before. The house full of movement. I stretch wide, let out one loud yawn, and roll off the bed like a man who has nothing but time. Which of course was not true at all.

My little brother Anil burst through the door with his usual theatrics. Shirt half button, hair sticking up like electric shock.

"You late, Pops!" he shouted, dramatic like the headmaster. "Miss Sehdat go write yuh up again!"

I smirked, rubbing my eyes. "Write me up for what? Graduating?"

He stomped away like a vex goat.

"You think you special cause a your last day? Bet next week you go back fi visit Miss Chin and carry flowers fi one gyal."

I flung my pillow at him and he dodged it.

"Don't mek me chase you, Anil."

But I don't chase. I get up slow, same way I always do, stretch, scratch, rinse face under the pipe outside, and hum one chutney tune while running the water.

Mama call from the kitchen, "Wear the white shirt. Iron it. Is not Bend Down Market we going. Today is the last day for you."

I sighed. I was done with school now. Now I join my older brother and father in the workforce.

In the mirror, I grinned at my reflection. The shirt fit precise. I look good. School done. Real work. Real life. Others probably have to worry about exams and university, but I already had three jobs lined up: welding, carpentry, and the cigarette factory with my older

brother. I was skilled with my hands, like Ba. Jack of all trades, master of none. But I liked it that way.

On the way out, Anil tried to follow me like him shadow.

"I coming too, Pops."

"Go brush yuh teeth, your mouth hot like pepper tea."

He glared at me, then grinned. He flicked water on me from the bucket. I chased him two steps for sport, then let him go. I always tease him, but I love the little runt. He used to sleep beside me in the thunderstorms, hold my hand when we pass cemetery. Every time he stands in the mirror perfecting his side swoop, I just tussle it and get him cross. I am proud of him, but I never tell him. Not out loud.

At school, the teacher call my name last. I'm not surprised. She said I have promise, if only I would stop talking. The class clapped, I bowed like a gentleman, and someone shout, "Tek yuh mouth to Parliament, Shower need you." I exit stage like movie star.

By the time I reach home, the sun high and my shirt damp with sweat. Mama waiting with food, Ba with silence. The others look at me different, like I cross some line they still waiting to reach. Even my older sister and

her kids were here. Everyone looked happy; they didn't say it, but it showed.

After dinner, we sat outside. I played my drum, tapping slow rhythms while Ma hummed her favorite bhajan. The younger children played with a flashlight and my sisters sat on the veranda chatting up a storm as usual. My older sister handed me a sugar roti wrapped in cloth.

"Where you working first?"

"I am thinking of joining the carpenter in Rollington Town, making my own hours. Or I might join big bro at the cigarette factory. I am undecided between the two."

"As long as you keep your head straight, heart soft, and come home to your family."

She look proud as she rubbed my head. It reminded me of the days I ran to her for everything. Before she was married. Before she became a Mrs. Now she belongs to another home, another family, and has children of her own. Percy and Amara. My favorite people in the world. My nephew is my wingman, and my niece is the apple of my eye.

I nodded, tapped my drum. "Family? I'm not looking a wife yet, sis."

She smiled, brushing my hair back like I was eight years old in her arms again.

"I know. That's why I'm not worried, Pops."

That night, after the house had finally gone still, Mama was humming low in the room with the younger babies and her grandchildren. Anil had knocked out on the mat, limbs flung like a starfish. I was outside, back resting against the water tank, watching the moon hang low like it had stories too. I was beating a soft rhythm, not even thinking, just letting it speak.

Then I hear Ba's footsteps. Soft but firm. I know that pace anywhere. He didn't say anything at first. Just lowered himself onto the low stone bench beside me, let out that deep tired sigh. The sigh that comes from a place far deeper than the lungs. We sat in silence for a bit, the only sound was crickets and the far-off bark of a dog down the lane.

"You play like my father," he finally said, voice low and even. "He used to beat tassa drum same way. He would make the ancestors dance with one hand and cry with the other."

"Maybe I got his spirit," I smirked.

Ba chuckled. His English was still fairly new, but he knew what I meant. "You have more than that. You have his stubbornness too. But you soft inside. You get that from Ma."

We sat in silence until I couldn't take it. I turned to him. "Ba, why you never talk about India much anymore?"

He paused, then scratched his beard like he was pulling the words out from under it. "The more I talk, the more it slip away. Like sand through fingers. It's there, and then gone. We never went back. Not cause we didn't want to. They just… they made it hard. Made it feel like we was better off here. So we build life in a place that never fully welcome us."

I didn't know what to say. For all the mischief I gave him, I never liked seeing the pain in Ba's face. He glanced at me, eyes dark and deep like cane fields at midnight.

"But you must remember. All of you. Don't let them take it from you. Your name, your roots, your pride. Don't be like me. The moment I stepped off that ship, my name was changed to a name they could pronounce. You born here, yes. But your blood is still Bhojpuri. Still Ganges

and coconut leaf. Still the same as the ones who crossed the kala pani before you."

I nodded, quiet. For once, no smart answer from my side.

I still remember the days Ba would keep us under the mango trees and share stories of India, hymns, bhajans, teach us how to play the dholak. I still longed for those days to return.

Lost in my own thoughts, I felt something I had not felt in a long time. Ba did something rare. He put his hand on my shoulder. Big, calloused, strong. And he squeezed.

"You are going to be alright. You are the most like me. You have fire. You just need focus. You think you a jack of all trades, but you don't even know yet what trade your heart will choose. Don't rush, but don't waste either."

He looked at me long. No smile, just a blink and a nod.

"I was proud of you the day you fix the lantern without being asked. And the day you built the shelves for your Ma. The day you stood up for your sisters. The day you taught your nephew how to ride a bike. And today, when you walk across the stage and complete your schooling."

I looked down, trying to hide the smile breaking over my face.

"Love you, you know," I said.

He said nothing. Just patted my back twice and stood. That was enough. That was his way.

And when he walked away, I sat there, looking up at that big moon, and I felt full. Not with food. Not with jokes. But with something older. Something deeper. Like legacy had finally touched my shoulder too.

CHAPTER 3 OUT FOR DUCKS

I was the one who fixed broken radios with a bent spoon and a matchstick, who patched the roof in exchange for sweet bread, who once got caught tying firecrackers to my smaller brother's pants tail.

By the time I was out of school, the mischief gave way slightly to something more focused. Ambition maybe, or just a hunger to do something of my own. That summer, I got a job with my older brother as a clerk at the cigarette factory in Kingston near the harbor. It wasn't grand, but it was something. I wore secondhand shirts with starched cuffs, carried my lunch in a tiffin wrapped in newspaper, and practiced my penmanship until the loops in my g looked like sails. I learned quickly how to read a ledger, how to slip a bribe to a customs officer without getting caught, and how to tell when a man was bluffing about a shipment of cigarettes.

The older clerks called me "fix-it" because I could sort a file, calm an angry client with jokes, and fix any equipment.

1955. That was the year Kingston felt electric, like the island was holding its breath and dancing at the same time.

Rocksteady hadn't taken over yet, but mento bands still made hips sway, and the rum never ran dry.

I was on the veranda cleaning mud off my cricket shoes when I heard the door creak open like it nervous. I saw my big brother, the walking rulebook, step out, looking left and right like him planning fi escape from jail. He had on his good shirt, the white one Ma iron and fold just so. Pants pressed, hair neat. But the giveaway? Him cologne. Heavy. Like he bathe in it.

I raised my eyebrows, trying not to laugh.
"So, where you going dressed like first-of-month money?"

Him jump, clutching his chest.
"You trying to kill me?"

"Nah," I said grinning. "Just trying to figure out if the world ending tonight. Cause the golden boy a sneak out."

He rolled his eyes but couldn't hide the smirk.
"There is a party in Bower Lane. Get dressed. Some of the boys from the factory going too, some from the university as well."

I nod slowly, dramatic.
"Girls, you say? Oh-ho, you finally grow teeth? Gwan then. Live a likkle yes."

He sighed, adjusted his shirt.
"I'm tired of being good and boring. Tired of watching life from the veranda. You always out there, laughing, playing. And me? I just read, study, stay out of trouble. But tonight… I want to feel what free feel like."

That stopped me in my tracks. I never hear him talk like that. I clap my hand on his shoulder.
"Then come, big bro, I'll take you. But you have to do exactly as I say."

"Like what?" he said.

"Like don't wear those stiff shoes. You can't dance in funeral shoes. Borrow mine."

He swap quick. Then I made him roll his sleeves up, loosen the collar. Add just a dash of coconut oil on his temples.
"Not too much, you not curry goat."

We sneak out through the back gate, tiptoe past Papa sleeping by the open window. I look at him, whisper, "Don't trip, you nuh build for licks like me."

He checked under his breath, shaking his head. "This feel illegal."

"That how you know it worth it," I whisper.

The sound hit us before the lights. Mento rhythms, big laugh, bigger bass. Smoke in the air. Jerk pan blazing. People moving like the whole street catch fire.

Raj froze. “IT’S LOUD.”

“It’s life,” I said, dragging him in.

Girls from uptown and downtown. Boys in slacks and shirtsleeves. A woman with eyes like danger waved at me. I waved back. Raj blinked like he saw colour for the first time.

Then out of nowhere, a girl walk past. Bright red skirt, gold hoops, hips like rhythm itself. She glanced our way and smile. My brother nearly faint.

“She smiled at you, not me,” I teased. “Look what happen when you stop hiding behind your books and bossing your siblings around.”

He swallowed hard. “What do I do now?”

“You walk over. You say something simple. Compliment her laugh. Then dance. Or… try to.”

My brother look like he would explode. But he did it. And I swear, when they started dancing, he was stiff at first, but by the second song he move free. Looser. And for once, the serious son of Raj and Asha was just another boy in the street. Just another heartbeat in the bassline.

Later that night, walking home under the fading moon and rising sun, he turn to me and say, "THANK YOU."

I grin. "Careful, I might turn you into me."

"Don't push it," he laugh. "But tonight… I remembered I'm young. And it felt good."

The house was too quiet. That kind of eerie quiet where even the flies know something coming. Me and Raj Jr. slip through the gate just before sunrise, shoes dusty, collars loose, smiles still lingering from the party. We were glowing.

Until we open the back door.

Mama was sitting at the table. Not standing. Sitting. Which was way worse. Head tie on tight. Elbows planted. One hand stirring bush tea like it was a potion for vengeance. She didn't even look up. Just said, calm and deadly, "So unu enjoy unu self, yes?"

I froze. Raj nearly walked out the door. I elbow him. "She talking to both of us. Answer."

"Ma," Raj stammered, "I… well… it was just—"

She slam the spoon down.
"YOU, RAJ. My good one. You now creeping round back gate like night thief? With Pops? Suppose the families of suitable unwed women see unu?"

I grinned. I couldn't help it. "Ma, he just needed to stretch him wings a likkle. No badness, just dance and music."

"Music?" she shouted. "You think dance and wine feed belly? You think reputation don't matter? You is big boy now, yes? Both of you want to play man, then go wash out the pit. Since you so free, go free it up."

Ba came to the door, shirt off, towel over his shoulder. He look at us long. Then raised one eyebrow. "What time unu reach home last night?"

"We got home this morning," I said with a smirk.

Raj said nothing, just rubbed the back of his neck like it could save him from judgement.

Ba did not raise his voice. He never did. Just said, "So you old enough fi party. From now on, yuh wake up five a.m. and help me clean the chicken coop every Sunday, since the street sweet you."

I groaned. Raj looked like he aged ten years in ten seconds.
"Yes, Ba," we mumbled in unison.

Ma wasn't done. She stood now, hand on hips. "And don't think of carrying your nephew or Anil out with unu. Just because you leave school don't mean nothing. You still have a name to protect. Your sisters need suitors."

Later that morning, Raj and I were knee deep in chicken mess, sweating, half dead, but laughing.
"Would you do it again?" I asked.

He thought. Then nodded. "Yes. But next time you dealing with the old lady's mouth alone."

"Fair," I said.

Two Weeks Later

It was two weeks after the party and the donkey pen fall out. By then me and Raj Jr. had settled into our Sunday sentence, shoveling dung, washing down the pens, and feeding the stubborn mule Papa swore was a blessing from Vishnu. I was convinced it was a punishment from somewhere else.

Sun hot like country pepper. Sweat dripping from my forehead into my eyes. And there was Raj with his sleeves rolled, shirt stuck to his back, looking like every bit of the man he never thought he'd be. No books. No chalkboard. Just dirt and muscle.

"Yuh nuh regret the party?" I asked, tossing a bucket of water over the floor.

He smirked. "Not the party. Just the smell."

I laughed. "Well now you know freedom come with stink."

We kept working a while, till the heat mellowed and we sat on the back step, barefoot and bruised, sharing coconut water straight from the shell.

"You ever think about settling down?" Raj asked, staring out at the breadfruit tree.

I blinked. "Settle with who? You know how much trouble one woman is? Two if you count the old lady."

He chuckled. "I see the way you look at girls though."

I shrugged. "I have had eyes for many girls. The bartender's wife, that girl from school, the shopkeeper's daughter, Miss Gloria niece from Mandeville."

Raj shook his head. "You nuh easy at all, Pops."

"Nah," I said. "I'm just curious. Women, them not like we. They carry weight in their eyes and rules in their hands. One minute them smile at you, next minute them a mek noise because you don't remember them favorite color."

"Kamla said I'm boring. But that girl I met at the party, she never ask about reading. She ask if I want to dance," Raj said.

"You like her?" I asked.

"Yes. I want to know if she'd still like me when the sun rises."

I tossed him a mango. "Find out then, nuh."

He caught it, peeled it with his teeth like how life taught us. Juice dripped down his chin.

"You nah settle down?" he said.

"Maybe. One day. If she can outdrink me in coconut water and outwit me in cricket," I replied.

"So never," he said, raising his coconut.

I raised mine back. "To women. Confusing, dangerous, and worth it."

We clinked shells. And in that moment, two brothers sat in sweat, stink, and sunlight, bound by blood, work, and the madness of falling in love in a world where both freedom and tradition had their price.

The following week went by slow as ever as I ready up for the big cricket match. This was the match.

The sun blazed that Saturday like it had something to prove. Ground dry and cracked, ball hard like debt to the shopkeeper, and every man itching to show who really run things. Franklin Town versus Papine. It was more than a match. It was war with sweat and style.

Long time I been wanting to shut up the uptown boys. Jerome and I reach early, bat slung over my shoulder, pockets full of jokes, confidence loud like kettle boiling over. The field was a dusty stretch of land behind Mr. Choy's shop, with trees for boundaries and zinc for shade. Boys from both sides were already stretching, imitating the West Indies team.

That's when I saw the pretty boy from Papine. Barrington. Tall. Clean jersey. White shoes. Hair slick like he soak it in pomade and prayer. And right beside him? Trouble. A girl. Not just any girl. Pretty skin, long skirt, fitted blouse, eyes that scan the crowd like she above it. She had bangles on both wrists and a smirk like she knew hearts could be broken.

Jerome and Raj leaned in. “Bwoy bring queen fi watch him play? Brave or fool.”

They won the toss and decided to bat first. Pretty boy walk out second, head high, trying to impress. He nod to his side before taking crease like him walking into Buckingham. I noticed the girl rolling her eyes like she bored already.

I stepped up to bowl. Jerome whisper, “Buss him head.” I grinned.

First ball: slow and wide. Let him get cocky. He step forward, miss. She laughed in the back, hiding her face. He adjusted his gloves.

Second ball: I wind up like me play for all my glory. Fast and flat. It bounce low, hit him pad dead on. Franklin Town bawl “HOWZAT” before the umpire even blink.

Out clean. First duck of the day. Papine princess looked shocked. I noticed a familiar look between him and her, but I paid it no mind.

He stood there confused like him just see duppy. I walk past him, pat his back. "Better luck next time. You can still shine off the field."

We chanted, "OUT FOR DUCKS, OUT FOR DUCKS," echo bouncing off every fence from here to Elleston Road. Uptown prince sulk off, kicking dust. The girl? She laugh. She spent the rest of the match under the almond tree, sipping coconut and talking to the other Papine girls.

Papine crumbled after that, bowled out cheap. We chased the runs easy, with Jerome hitting six to end it in style. We dance on the field like it was a stage show, barefoot and bold. The zinc fence never heard such niceness.

On the way out, I exchanged nods with Barrington. A sign of respect. Jerome nudged me. "You really had to embarrass the man in front of she?"

I winked. "This is cricket. This is war. And mi aim nuh miss when pride deh pon the line."

The following Sunday was Hussay. Although we practice Hindu customs, we still showed support for our Muslim brothers. That night of Hussay, the whole street came alive. People from all over east and west Kingston showed up. Oil lamps flicker, incense curling sweet and sharp in the air.

CHAPTER 3 OUT FOR DUCKS

Tassa drums pound like heartbeat on fire. Paper crescent moons and flags flap in the breeze, each one brighter than the next.

I was at the front of course, drumming. Drum strapped to my waist, palms chalked, sweat glistening off my brow. When I play tassa, my body forget the rules. Fingers fly, hips move in time, head bounce with rhythm.

Mama in the corner serving dhal and sweet rice. Ba in his kurta, solemn as ever, arms folded but nodding every now and then. My siblings liming by the juice cart.

My nephew Percy was buying a coconut from Juicy and I had to do a double take.

Yes. It was she. The same girl from the cricket field. I didn't see Papine prince with her though. She was alone.

When I saw her it was like the crowd blurred. She wore a mustard-colored sari that caught every flame. Gold bangles again. Same eyes. Hair in a honeycomb. I only know that term because of my sisters.

Those eyes. Watching everything and watching me.

I missed a beat on the drum. Just one. Jerome side-eye me, confused. "Yuh slipping?" he said.

I shook it off, picked the rhythm back up, and focused. She was standing beneath the almond tree sipping from a cup, playing with some smaller children. One came to her and held his hands up so she could pick him up. She lifted him, settled him on her hip like she was born for it.

Every few minutes our eyes met.

And what did I do? Nothing. Not a step. Not a smile. Not even a nod. Just kept playing, like the beat could hide me from whatever truth her presence stirred. Why? Maybe because I was tired of being the bold one. Maybe because I wanted someone else to make the first move. Or maybe I was scared. Scared that if I touched something real, it would vanish like smoke.

Later, when the crescent was lifted and the crowd roared, I noticed her walking next to Barrington and the little children. Soon they were gone. Slipped into the night like incense mist.

Raj noticed the exchange and said nothing. But later that night when I lay on my zinc roof staring up at the stars, drum still echoing in my fingers, I whispered to no one in particular, "She looked good in yellow."

CHAPTER 3 OUT FOR DUCKS

The morning after Hussay, the fire pot was still warm. The ashes still carried the scent of sweets and incense. Mama sat on the stool by the back door, peeling ginger for her tea. Her bangles clicked with every movement, but her eyes were far away, looking somewhere behind the trees, behind the years.

I stepped out barefoot, still shirtless from sleep. She didn't look at me right away. Just said, "You play the drum like it speaks for your heart."

I sat on the step beside her.
"Maybe it is."

"I watched you last night. And I watched all the girls eyeing you."

I looked down. Said nothing.

She dropped the slices of ginger into the boiling water. "You say nothing, but your silence loud, Pops."

"Mama, not everything that is pretty is meant to be touched."

She wiped her hands on her apron and finally looked at me. "You getting older now. You working. People watching. Good families asking. Daughters need husbands. Girls who can cook and pray and keep home steady."

"Steady don't mean happy," I said. "And happiness don't come from matchmaking."

Her jaw clenched but she stayed soft. "It come from building. Brick by brick. Not chasing wind. Your father and me, we were not arranged. We were lucky. But I still believe in tradition. It protect us. It hold us together."

I leaned back, let the sun warm my face.
"Maybe I'm not ready to be held together yet."

She reached out, cupped my cheek, same way she did when I was small and crying over scraped knees.
"You are my moonlight, Pops. But even moon must rise."

I leaned into her hand. "Let me shine a likkle longer, Mama. Not ready to set just yet."

She didn't smile, but her fingers lingered. Then she stood, poured the tea, and said, "If you break tradition, you must be strong enough to build something better. Promise me you won't build alone."

I nodded, voice low.
"One day I'll build, Mama, when I find someone. If I don't, I'll stay with you and Ba."

She handed me the tea, kissed the top of my head, and whispered, "One day."

The week after Hussay passed like thick molasses. Nothing big happen, but every day left a different kind of dust on my skin. Same work. Same yard. Same arguments about who eat the last of the curry goat. But something was shifting. I could feel it.

On Monday, the radiator bust on Uncle Dinesh Morris' Oxford. I fixed it for him after work one day. I was sore, but pride intact.

I passed by Miss Bibi yard, and she gave me a wink with peanut cake. "You need fattening, child." I took it. Who was I to argue with wisdom and sugar?

By Tuesday Jerome showed up late, shirt inside out, love bite on his neck. The whole assembly line in the factory teased him till him red like sorrel.

"You a man now?" I shouted, ducking the greasy rag he fling at me.

Later while fetching some orders for the outgoing department, I heard my coworkers whispering about the Papine people.

"Them throwing something big this weekend. Some party. The Puran family, I think."

My ears perked. That name, I know it.

By Wednesday we had midweek rain. Cold and relentless. The kind that make zinc sound like judgment day. Work slow. Mama send containers of dhal and aloo to the factory with Percy, my nephew. I ate every last drop. No shame.

By Thursday the buzz around the Papine party get louder. Jerome said he might go because of his cousin. He asked if Raj and I want to go. I was undecided.

Friday became the longest workday. Two customers argued over their orders. Raj lost his temper. Percy walked to the factory to ask me to fix his bike. My niece asked me to build her one too. It was like the work never ended that day.

After I locked up the tool shed, I sat on the step out back, black grease in the creases of my fingers, staring at the streetlights. A little boy passed with a cricket bat too big for him, dragging it like legacy. I thought of Ba. Of my sisters. Of my old lady. And of the girl in the mustard sari.

And I thought, maybe this life is not about one big moment. Maybe it is about the little ones. The fried peanut. The scolding. The silence. The late bus ride home. Maybe I was building something without realizing.

Raj came to fetch me at the tool shed.
"You in for the Papine party tomorrow?"

I already knew my answer.

Papine never felt like my place. Too neat. Too proud. People didn't shout from veranda to street. They waved polite, like they afraid to disturb the breeze. Even the dogs barked different. But Jerome, Raj, and I dragged ourselves to the party one Saturday night, and curiosity is always sweeter than caution.

The house was big, two stories, columns at the front, garden with plumeria and a view that stretch all the way to Blue Mountains. I tighten my belt and told myself to behave.

The music inside was a blend of mento, soul, and ska. Something magical, like all the roads we came from finally meeting in one yard. Lights string across the trees. Girls in chiffon and gold. Boys leaning on banisters. And then I saw her.

She wasn't laughing. She wasn't clapping or fixing her sari. She was dancing. Not wild. Not dramatic. Just free. Hands up. Eyes closed. Hips moving like she knew rhythm personally.

I froze. Drink in hand. For all the girls I winked at, flirted with, charmed, this one made me forget how to breathe. And before I could even stop myself, I turned to Jerome. "That's her."

He looked. "Who, Barrington sister?"

I blinked. "His what?"

"His sister, man. I just found out at Hussay. He not that good looking to get someone like she. She's the younger sister. She work at the restaurant with him."

I stared at her again, the pieces falling into place like domino. Her laughing at Barrington's mistakes. Her standing alone at Hussay. The familiar eyes. The way she looked through me, not at me. Not taken. Untouched.

She opened her eyes mid song. And for a split second, they landed on mine.

No smile. Just awareness. Like she felt me before she saw me.

I looked away first. Me. The mouthy one. The charmer. The show-off. I looked away.

The music changed. Someone passed me a drink. Jerome said something about fried fish in the kitchen. But everything was background now. My whole body was heat and hesitation.

I didn't walk up to her. Not yet. I stayed at the edge of the party, watching her shine in a place that belonged to her. Not me. This was her stage. And me? I was the boy who finally realized, maybe I didn't need to chase this girl. Maybe I needed to earn the right to stand beside her.

I made my way over slow, pretending not to be nervous. I'd faced teachers, police, and Ma in rage, but none of them made my palms sweat like this girl standing in Papine.

"You again," she said, one eyebrow raised.

"Me again," I replied, clearing my throat.

She laughed, like she had been holding it in for days.
"I heard you bowled my brother out on purpose."

"Guilty," I said.

"Good," she answered. "He needed humbling."

The music shifted, softer now. She turned to walk away.

"Wait!" I nearly shouted. "Do you want to dance? I'm better at dancing than cricket."

I held my hand out, and to my surprise, she took it.

My feet moved before my brain caught up. Suddenly, I was in the middle of the crowd, palm on her waist, her hand resting light on my shoulder. Not pressed tight—just enough. Enough to feel everything.

She danced smooth, effortless. I tried to match her rhythm, heart thudding so loud, I swore it drowned the bassline.

"You never told me your name," she said mid-spin.

"It's complicated. Comes with charm, danger, and a mama who still beat my backside."

She rolled her eyes. "Try me."

So I told her. Real name. Full name. The one people only use when it matters.

"Mhm," she said, testing the syllables. "It suits you. My name is Devi."

I smiled. "I know. I wouldn't dance with a stranger."

Later, I slipped out by the mango tree to catch some air. Felt a hand tap my shoulder. It was Barrington.

"You bowl me out the other day?" he asked.

I stiffened, ready for blows. But he only extended his hand. We shook—mutual respect sealed in calluses.

After that, I couldn't help it. I looked for her everywhere. Even turned down dances from two well-known girls in our crowd. Raj and Jerome side-eyed me like they'd never seen me act this way. But I just wanted to be near her. Talking or not. Dancing or not. Her presence was enough.

Soon Raj and Jerome came to fetch me. "We need to get back downtown before Ma and Ba realize."

I sighed, turned to her. "So when will I see you again?"

She tilted her head, lips curling like she enjoyed this game. "Depends," she said low, "you plan on bowling out the rest of my brothers?"

"Only if they stand between me and you," I grinned.

She looked away at the dancers, then back at me with calm, knowing eyes.

"Kingston small," she said. "You'll find me if you really want to."

"That's not a yes," I pressed.

“It’s not a no,” she replied.

She didn’t kiss me. Didn’t ask for my address. No contact details. She didn’t ask for anything. Just touched my wrist and said, “Next time, don’t wait so long to speak.”

Then she slipped back into the crowd, her bangles chiming like a promise.

I walked home under the stars that night. Not drunk. Not dazed. Just…different. Like something shifted inside me. Like the rhythm I’d been chasing finally had a name.

Our exchange stretched for hours, but it felt like minutes. And for the first time in my life, a woman left me standing there like a batsman bowled first ball—out for ducks. Except this time, it wasn’t shame I felt. It was awe.

CHAPTER 4 DAHL FROM PAPINE

By Monday morning, the whole crew at work had something to say. I barely walked in and Jerome and Raj already flinging paper at me like we in some kind of lovers' quarrel.

"So what really going on with you and Barry sister?" Jerome asked, smirking.

"You two dance like you been writing love letters since primary school."

"Must be serious," Raj added. "You didn't flirt with anyone else at the party. I don't see you make talk to no one since then."

I chuckled, tried to play it off.

"She dance, I dance. People dancing. Is a party, not a proposal."

"Yeah, but you never look at any girl like that before," Jerome said. "You look like you saw the Ganges river in her eyes."

I wiped my hands and bent over the ledger, anything to avoid their stares.

"She different."

"Different how?" Raj pressed.

"Like she don't need to try. She don't chase attention. She just stand there, and everything else move round her. I don't even know if she like me, or if I'm just the clown who can make she laugh every now and then."

Jerome leaned on the bench. "So what's the next move then, lover man?"

I smirked. "Well, I can go pick up lunch from the shop if you hungry."

I decided to give it a few days before I journey to her family's place. I didn't want to scare the girl. Besides, Ma would disown me if I wasted the lunch she packed for me.

Later that day, walking home with the sun low and the sky pink like guava flesh, I sat on the rocking chair on the veranda, the weight of the day heavy in my back. Before I could even take off my shoes, I heard them coming—barefoot thunder down the hallway. My nephew and niece.

"Yuh look mash up," Percy said.

"I feel mash up," I replied.

"Hard day, Uncle Pops?" Amara asked, settling beside me.

"Every day hard, but it still sweet. Tired, not broken."

They nestled on either side of me, like it was some ritual we all knew by heart.

"Yuh want to leave Jamaica, Uncle Pops?" Percy asked.

I side-eyed him. That question wasn't random. Kids don't ask things for fun.

"Plenty people go foreign, chasing money and comfort. But I don't know. Here…here is where my heart feel warm, even when my pocket cold. Plus, who going take care of your granny if I leave—and your miserable mother?"

"I don't want to leave, Uncle," Amara said softly.

I rubbed her hair, looking at her eyes. Same eyes as my older sister once had, before she gave up her own wings for marriage.

"Jamaica is story. And we living in the middle chapter. Rain, fire, mango, music—everything here come with a memory."

"Love is here too. People argue. People leave," Percy said.

That one catch me deep in the chest. These children—always watching, hearing more than people think.

"Love everywhere. Love hard. Love endure. You ever see two old people cussing on the veranda, then share roti five minutes later? That's Jamaican love. Stubborn and sweet."

"That's Mama and Papa," Amara said.

"Exactly."

We sat quiet for a moment, sky above us fading from orange to indigo. Somewhere down the lane, a mento song played low on the radio.

"Family not always easy. But if you lucky, it give you roots. And when you get old like me, you realize roots more important than wings."

"Gwan fly, Uncle. But fly low, so we can catch up to you," Percy said.

I looked at him and nearly cry. Not cause I was sad. But because love was right there—on a quiet veranda, with dusty boots, tired arms, and two little hearts reminding me who I really was.

The rest of the week passed in a blur of endless ledgers, angry customers, Ma's scolding, and loud children in my yard. But every spare moment, my mind drifted back to that time under the fairy lights, her eyes holding mine like they'd been waiting since birth.

When Friday finally came, I put on my cleanest shirt, combed my hair twice, and told Ma she didn't have to pack lunch for me. I would pick something up.

She was the middle child—just like me. Maybe that's why I couldn't stop thinking about her. In families like ours, middle children become many things: peacemakers, quiet rebels, second mothers, invisible backbones. She carried all of it like she was born to balance weight no one else saw.

She had too many siblings to count on one hand. Three brothers older, two sisters older, and three sisters younger who followed her like shadows. Still, she managed it all—schoolbooks, housework, temple duties—without ever raising her voice. Everyone in Papine knew her as "Barry Sister," but she was much more. She could flip a roti with one hand, stir dhal with the other, and still have enough grace left to offer you water with a smile that meant something only if she wanted it to.

The first time I saw her again wasn't at a party or a cricket field. It was at the restaurant she ran with her brother. A small cookshop near the Papine roundabout. I went at lunch.

Took the bus from the factory, north instead of home, skipping Ma's food just this once.

There she was, behind the counter, apron tied tight, steam rising like she lived in another world.

She didn't look surprised. Didn't flinch or flutter. Just raised one eyebrow like she'd been expecting me.

"You want to order something—or are you just here to stare?" she asked, ladle in hand.

"Both," I said. "In that order."

She rolled her eyes, scooped curry chicken and rice, and walked away before I could even ask for extra pepper. That was her way. No softness for free. But the curry? Hot, rich, and tasting like something I hadn't even known I was missing.

It wasn't the food that brought me back three more times that week. It was her. Each time I walked in, she acted like she didn't notice me. Never called my name. Never smiled first. Just slid the plate across the counter and disappeared into the back. But every visit, her hand lingered a second longer, her eyes stayed a moment too long.

So the following week, I got creative. I brought backup.

My nephew Percy, ten years old, pocket full of sweetie and badness, became my postman. I slipped him a note with my order: *"Tell her it's for the pretty girl who act like she don't know me."*

He winked, ran inside bold, and handed it over. She read it, looked up at Percy, then out the window—straight at me. No smile. Just an unimpressed stare. Then she shook her head and handed him a napkin.

Percy came back grinning. "She say, tell your uncle his charm stale like old dumpling."

I laughed so loud a dog barked from the corner.

That became our routine. Me showing up with fake errands. Percy delivering notes that weren't really notes, just excuses. And her answering without ever giving more than a line or two. But the food came warmer. The glances lingered. Her fingers brushed mine across the counter, like it was an accident.

One day Percy came out, hands in his pockets.

"She nuh give me no note this time, Uncle Pops."

"So she tired of me already?" I asked.

“Nah.” He smirked. “She say if you want to talk to her, stop using a child. Come Sunday when the shop slow. But only if you buying something real. No more fake errands.”

I nodded, heart jumping quiet in my chest.
“Sunday it is.”

When the day came, I asked my sister to comb my hair and told Percy, “You off duty. I’m going in myself.”

The shop was quiet, just like she promised. No long line. No yelling for extra pepper. No smell of saltfish and sweat pressing on the air. Just the slow simmer of dhal in the back, sunlight through the dusty jalousie window, and the soft scrape of a spoon against a pot.

She was wiping the counter when I walked in. Didn’t look up right away. Like she already felt me before the door even opened.

“So,” she said, still working the cloth, “you finally decide to face me like a man instead of hiding behind Percy and curry orders.”

“I had to build up the courage,” I said. “Your spirit dangerous, but calm.”

“So is your handwriting.”

This time she looked up properly. No smirk. No teasing. Just steady eyes, like she'd been waiting for me to mean it.

"I came because I wanted to see the real you," I said. "Not the one behind the counter. Not the girl under fairy lights. You."

She leaned against the wall, arms crossed. Not cold—just cautious.
"And what do you think the real me is?"

"Someone who move quiet but carry thunder. Who got ten people leaning on her and still find space to breathe. Someone who laugh with her whole mouth but guard her heart like it holy."

She blinked. Not surprised. Just… seen.

"You talk like a man who want something. What is it?"

"I want time. I want to know how you stir your dhal so smooth. I want to know if you kept my notes in your apron pocket. I want to know you."

She laughed, shaking her head. "You nuh give up easy, do you?"

"Not when something worth the trouble."

A long pause. Then she pulled out a chair, sat across from me. No more games. Just presence.

“Fine. You want to talk? Sit. Eat. And don’t try charm your way with me. Just be real.”

She slid a bowl toward me. Curry pumpkin, dhal, roti. Steam rising like prayer.

And just like that—between turmeric and tension, between past jokes and future questions—we began. We talked until the sun dipped low, until I forgot the time.

By the time I got home, the sky was pink as guava flesh. I barely reached the veranda before I heard the thunder of bare feet.

Percy and Amara burst in.

“So what she say?” Percy demanded.

“Good evening to you too,” I said, grinning.

“Yuh don’t even let Uncle Pops breathe,” Amara giggled.

“I’ve been waiting all day!” Percy whined.

I pulled him into a headlock, careful not to crush his shirt. “Thank you, my little postman. Mission complete. We had a good talk today. I learned a lot.”

“She must like you then,” Percy said smug. “Girls always pretend they don’t like you, but they do.”

“Oh? You’re a real ladies’ gentleman now?” I teased.

Amara climbed onto the chair arm, chin resting on me. She didn’t tease, didn’t grin. Just asked softly, “Is she nice?”

I paused. Not for the answer, but for the weight of her question.

“She is,” I said. “She looks you in the eye when she talks. She doesn’t laugh just to be polite. And she knows how to make dhal smooth and clap roti firm. Essential skills.”

Amara tilted her head. “You should marry someone who makes you softer, Uncle Pops. Not someone who makes you small.”

That pierced deeper than any joke. Eight years old, but her words carried centuries. I kissed her forehead and pulled her close.

“You keep talking like that and I’ll never let you grow up.”

“Good! Cause when she start dating, I go need backup,” Percy added.

We laughed together, loud and whole. And in that small moment—under the peeling veranda, tired from work, full from food—I didn't feel restless. Just full.

After that Sunday, nothing was the same. And nothing was rushed. She didn't give me answers in full sentences, but in smaller things.

A glance. A walk shared halfway to the bus stop. A second roti slipped in with my order.

The following Saturday, I convinced her to meet me by the waterfront. Percy played postman again—this time bribed with sweetie and extra pocket change to deliver my "letter."

It was early evening, sea breeze sharp with salt, the sky glowing pawpaw-orange. Vendors lined the pier: fried fish crackling in hot oil, pineapple slices dusted with salt, barefoot boys offering shoe shines.

"Why you wanted me to meet you here?" she asked.

"Because I like seeing things move. And because I wanted to know if you ever just…let go."

She smirked. "This is me letting go. I'm outside with you, aren't I?"

We sat at the edge, feet swinging over the rocks. She told me about growing up in Tavern, then Papine—with a mother who never sat still and brothers who never sat quiet. I told her about York Street, about a house full of noise and opinion, and how I felt most myself on rooftops or cricket fields.

She admitted she once wanted to be a teacher. But life had other plans. She stayed to help her brother run the restaurant. People crossed Kingston just to taste her cooking.

Another day, I walked with her through Coronation Market. The air was a storm of yam dust, ginger, sugarcane, sweat. She bargained sharp with a vendor for guava, then handed me one like it was treasure.

"If you can peel it with your thumb and not bruise the flesh, maybe I'll share another Sunday with you."

"You using fruit as a test now?"

"Every woman does. You just catching on late."

On a quieter day, we wandered Hope Gardens. She kicked off her shoes, toes in the grass, talking about how flowers bloom whether or not people notice. I couldn't stop noticing her.

“You don’t say much, you know,” I said.

“That’s because men like you say enough for both of us.”

“But I want to hear you.”

She turned, eyes steady. “Then listen with more than your big ears.”

That’s how it was. No grand declarations. No fireworks. Just dhal and roti, sidewalk walks, mango trees, second glances, and conversations that ran like rivers—slow, bending, steady. With every day, every hour stolen from the world, I stopped chasing her and started meeting her where she was.

A doll from Papine.

Meanwhile, on York Street…

“He not even eating proper these days,” Mama muttered, tasting the pot. “Gone before breakfast, come back after dinner. And when I ask him where him been, all he say is ‘out.’ Out where? With who? Cricket season done.”

She shook her head, added more salt. Not angry—just unsettled. A mother always knows when her child start giving his heart to someone else. She just don't always know to who.

Ba didn't say much. Just watched his son from the corner of his eye when he passed through the yard whistling. Whistling. That boy never whistled unless he was hiding mischief—or something sweeter.

"You look like man who get good sleep," Ba said one afternoon, not looking up.

"I do," I replied, brushing dirt off my shoes.

"Must be nice," he said, leaving it there. But he noticed the fresh shirt. The combed hair. The quiet new weight in his son's voice—the kind that only comes when a man start walking in two worlds: his home, and his heart.

Shanti and Kamla sat folding clothes on the veranda.

"I know that look," Shanti said, shaking out a shirt. "That's the look of somebody pretending to be tired when really they hiding something sweet."

"You think he meet someone?" Kamla asked.

Shanti smirked. "He meet someone long time now. But now it serious. He walking like him listening to music nobody else hear."

Under the mango tree, Percy and Amara reached for the juiciest fruit but were distracted by their uncle's new demeanor.

"He acting weird," Percy said.

"No. He acting happy," Amara corrected.

"Same thing."

They laughed, but from then on, they watched the gate more. Waiting to see when he'd come back. Wondering what world he was building outside the family—and if they'd be invited in.

I didn't know when exactly it happened. When the girl behind the counter become more than a pretty face in mustard colored silk. Maybe it was the way she stirred her pot, slow and steady like memory itself. Or the way she never let me have anything easy, not a smile, not a story, not even extra pepper. There was something in the way she held back that made me lean in, and something in the way she gave piece by piece, that made me want to stay. She wasn't like the other girls. She wasn't fireworks and flash. She was a quiet flame, and somehow I found myself warming my hands by her without even realizing I was cold. The dhal from Papine wasn't just food, it was rhythm, ritual, resistance. It was a spoonful of softness in a hard world, a reminder that some things take time to boil, to thicken, to reach their flavor. And I who had always chased laughter, noise, and the next big thrill was suddenly slowing down. I was learning to listen with more than my big ears. And in the middle of Kingston, under almond trees and starlight, I was learning, maybe for the first time, how to love.

CHAPTER 5 BEYOND THE TEMPLE

The gate creaked like it always did, no matter how soft I tried to push it. Even the night couldn't keep my comings and goings a secret. The yard was dark except for the veranda light Mama always left on just in case. I knew better than to think it was accidental. That little glow meant I am watching. I know. Come inside still.

My shoes hit the steps with soft thuds. I sat for a second before opening the door, letting the air cool the warmth still clinging to my shirt, the scent of coconut oil still clinging to my sleeves where she leaned against me in the market. My fingers still smelled faintly of mango and ink. Hers.

I didn't hear Mama until she cleared her throat.

"You eat already?"

Her voice from inside. Not angry. Just there. Like God during a storm.

"Yes Ma. I ate. Real food."

"Better be real food. You getting skinny Pops. And don't think I didn't notice you miss two of your sister's suitor meetings."

Kamla was finally ready to be arranged and the suitors were lining up left, right, and center for the chance to audition.

I walked inside. She was in her chair, knitting something that did not need to be knitted, just so her hands had something to do while her mind worked over me like laundry.

"I'll help Kamla tomorrow. I promise."

She looked at me. Not hard, not soft. Just looked. Like she was trying to read something under my skin.

"Pops you not drifting, are you?"

"No Ma. I'm still your favorite. I'm floating a little."

She nodded. That was enough for now. In our house, silence was sometimes louder than shouting. I kissed her forehead, whispered goodnight, and went to wash the day off my hands.

In the hallway, I caught glimpse of Ba in his undershirt smoking his pipe quietly. He didn't say a word. Just gave me one small nod. A man's way of saying I see you. I hope you know what you're doing.

And I nodded back. Because I didn't know exactly, but I was starting to.

The next morning the house was noisy. It is normally noisy, but today it was a good sign. It meant one thing. Kamla had made up her mind.

She was sitting cross legged on the floor, fanning herself, beaming like the rice was already thrown and the sari was already worn.

"I don't want a long courtship. Just someone decent. Temple raised, proper job. Ma already writing down names."

Shanti sat behind her, braiding her hair. "And what if he bald and bad breathed with a lazy eye?"

"If he respectful and steady, I can live with one eye watching east," Kamla said.

I walked in just in time to catch that line and dropped my tool bag with a thud.

"Is a man you marrying or a donkey? Steady and decent sound like mule qualities."

She threw a cushion at me with more force than expected.

“At least I’m not chasing riddles and skirts like you, waiting on some girl to blink twice before I get brave,” Kamla said.

I heard laughing from behind the curtain and saw Percy and Amara stick their heads out. Everyone laughed except Amara, who came and sat by my side, quiet as always. She didn’t say much, just rested her chin on my shoulder, watching the storm swirl around us.

“I think you want to be picked so you don’t have to choose Kamla,” Shanti said.

“Less pressure,” Raj Jr added.

“No, that’s not true,” Kamla replied.

“Maybe it is. Maybe it feel easier to follow the path already built than to dig your own in the mud.”

For a moment, there was quiet. That rare hush that came when we actually listened to each other.

“It’s not about easy. It’s about honour. Ma and Ba built this life from nothing. If they trust a match, who am I to question?” Kamla said.

I looked at her. Really looked. She wasn’t just giggling about saris and sweets. She was trying to make order out of the mess. Trying to belong to something bigger than herself.

And I couldn't help but to think of my older sister Riya, who wasn't even here for this talk.

Sometimes when we got quiet during our sibling talk, one of us would bring her up. Riya. She had been married since I was eight years old. I still remember the day she left us. Now she lived out in Clarendon with her husband's family, spending her days boiling water, nursing his father's legs, and making chai for a mother in law who never smiled. We didn't see her much anymore. She sent short letters folded in neat squares, full of polite news and none of her heart. She sent her heart to keep us company in the form of Percy and Amara.

Ma would say she is doing her duty, and Ba would nod, proud. But the rest of us weren't so sure. Shanti said she looked thinner the last time. Kamla said she looked tired. Raj said she is her husband's problem now. Anil hardly remembers her. And me? I couldn't forget how she took care of me like a mother. I couldn't forget the way she used to laugh before she left. Loud. Free. Like someone who didn't owe anyone anything yet.

Sometimes I wonder if she ever had a say. If she ever looked at her husband and thought, this is who I want to grow old with. Or if she just blinked one day and woke up in someone else's kitchen, serving someone else's life. Watching her disappear like that, bit by bit, letter by letter, it stayed with me. Marriage was always spoken about like an achievement in our house. A ticket to security, respect, tradition. But all I ever saw was women folding themselves smaller to fit inside other people's expectations.

And that is why Devi made me pause. She moved like no one owned her. She laughed when she meant it. She worked, but she never looked tired of giving. And somehow, she made me feel like I could be loved without shrinking, without pretending. Riya married into silence. I wanted something loud. Something real. And the more time I spent with Devi, the more I knew I wasn't willing to trade freedom for tradition, not even for a family that had given me everything.

Now hearing all this wedding talk from Kamla, I started to wonder. Was I not going to be able to make fun of her anymore? Was I not going to be able to steal the bread out of her hand as it made its way to her mouth?

As the days went on, marriage fever took over York Street.

The following Friday, the front room was filled with the scent of rose water and fresh linen. Mama had cleared the center table and laid out the suitor letters like sacred texts, folded sheets with temple stamps, family crests, and neat handwriting listing education, occupation, caste, complexion. Like Kamla was auditioning for a role in someone else's play.

She sat upright on the edge of the couch, sari tucked just right, trying to look calm, but her eyes kept darting to the side where Shanti, Raj, Anil, and I lounged like critics at a talent show.

"This one is from the Maharaj family. Their boy work in a bank. Steady job. Owns bicycles. Father is a pandit," Ma said.

I leaned forward. "Does he smile? Or is the bicycle the most joyful thing in the house?"

Kamla glared at me. "At least he has a future. Not everybody can charm their way through sweet talk like you."

Shanti tried to soften it. "He sound decent. But does he make you feel anything? Even nervous?"

Ma chimed in. "Nervousness not required. Stability is. You need someone with roots."

I looked at Kamla then. Really looked. She wasn't glowing. She wasn't miserable either. She was managing. Like she had made peace with the idea of being picked, as long as the picker was polite and had a savings account.

"Yuh nuh have to marry someone because they tick the boxes," I said.

"And end up like you? Floating around Papine with a girl who probably don't even know your full name," she snapped.

The room went quiet. Even Ma froze.

"He told her his name," Percy said softly.

Everyone looked at him. He was sitting on the floor doing arithmetic next to his sister, like he didn't just drop the heaviest truth in the room. Amara snorted. I tried not to smile.

Ma collected the letters. "No more tonight. We pray on it. Kamla will choose. But not with this racket in her ears."

As the room cleared, Kamla and I were the last to leave. She looked at me, not angry, just tired.

"I don't want perfect Pops. I just want peace."

“Then don’t settle. Even peace should feel like yours.”

She didn’t answer. Just walked off, the sound of her bangles soft but certain.

Later that evening after all the bang a rang we caused in the living room, Raj, Anil, Percy and I sat outside under the mango tree after bringing the goats back from the field.

“Me nah lie, mi nuh mind if Mama arrange mi ting. As long as she kind, can cook, and nuh too mouthy, mi good. Life nuh haffi be no big romance, mi just want calm,” Raj said.

“Calm? I cyan live in calm alone. I want noise. Fire. Someone weh can argue with me and still warm my food after. Love nuh come in a rice pot,” I said.

“I’m not doing none of that. Mi choosing my woman myself. Cant tell me fi marry a girl cause her father know how fi read Ramayan,” Anil perked up and said, which surprised all of us.

“You are a little boy Anil. You don’t even know how to wash your own socks. Love sweet til rent due and pickney sick. Is stability I want,” Raj interjected.

I looked between both of them. “But you can get stability and spark. Devi nuh drop from the sky. She real. She talk back. She watch me close, like she see me for true.”

“Here this Loverboy now. You tun inna poet and have Percy a deliver your letters?” Anil sneered.

Percy snickered.

“Watch your mouth. Me write because me cyan talk round she. Every time me see her, my tongue stammer like donkey.”

Raj laughed. “Still…the old lady nah go like this. She want we fi marry inside the temple, keep blood clean, keep tradition alive. You know how she stay.”

“Tradition cant feed my belly. I nuh plan fi live and dead inna somebody else shadow,” Anil said.

The rest of the night hang heavy. Crickets chirping like background singers. A dog bark in the distance. None of them spoke for a while, but all of them were thinking, even little Percy.

The next day after work I retreated to the cook shop. I passed Barrington on the corner and hailed him. He knew exactly where I was going, and his hail was his blessing.

It was just past twilight when I arrived. I found her leaning against the back wall of the shop, arms folded, apron still on, eyes soft with that kind of tired only women who work all day wear like jewelry. She saw me coming but didn't move. Just waited, like always, like she knew I had something sitting on my chest.

I went over the conversations I had with my family regarding Kamla.

"Just so? Pick a man? Like pick him from a breadfruit tree?" she asked.

"My sister said it is peace. I call it settling. But Mama proud. Letters flying, dowry whispering, Ba quiet and watching. It feel like everybody playing their role and I am just…drifting."

Devi didn't laugh. She didn't tease. She just tilted her head slightly like she was listening past the words, down into the ache beneath.

"You think your sister unhappy?"

"I think she scared. I think we all are. But some of us run and some of us kneel."

We stood there in the Kingston dusk, streetlights flickering, frying oil cooling in the shop behind her, and for the first time, I asked the question that had been burning since that first bowl of dhal.

“What about you? Your family…they ever try to arrange something for you?”

She leaned back, arms now loose at her side.

“No. Never.”

“Never,” I said.

“My father was indentured from Sindh. Came here young. He is Hindu. My mother is from Lahore. Muslim. They met on a plantation, of all places. Fell in love in the middle of cane stalk and cane knives. Family disowned both of them back home. But here? They built a life. A hard one. But full of choice.”

She looked away for a moment, her voice softer now.

“They raised us with both prayers in the house. Gita and Qur’an on the same shelf. And when my older sister married a Rasta man from Spanish Town, my mother cooked curry goat for the reception herself. When my brother brought home a maroon girl from Accompong, Daddy just nodded and said, at least she got spirit."

"So nobody try stop them?" I asked.

"They tried. But my parents already lost everything once. They had nothing left to protect but freedom."

I didn't answer. Just stared at her, that familiar heat rising in my throat. Not just desire, but respect. Deep, bone level respect.

"We do not marry to preserve bloodline. We marry to preserve joy. That what my mother always says." She added.

And I swear, in that moment, I wanted nothing more than to hold that kind of freedom in my hands. And maybe just maybe give it back to her in return.

The walk to Devi's house was longer than I expected, winding past the bus stand, up a gravel path near the foothills outside Papine, where breadfruit trees leaned like gossiping aunties and dogs barked at shadows for sport. She didn't say much on the way, just hummed something low and tuneless. I didn't mind. Her silence had rhythm to it.

When we reached the gate, a crooked wooden thing painted blue at the top, peeling from sun and time, she paused and looked at me.

"You can come in. But only on the veranda. Parents. You know."

I nodded. Stepped through the gate like I was crossing into a different version of Jamaica.

The yard smelled like jasmine and cumin. Curry leaf. Lime peel. But also ackee. Mint. Something baking. Everything mixed. Everything alive.

Children's voices rang out from the back, two little ones chasing each other around like a goat. Someone was strumming a four-string banjo near the window, badly but joyfully. Wind chimes clinked beside a flagpole that held no flag.

And on the veranda, her mother sat in a soft brown pleated skirt, feet tucked beneath her, reading something in Urdu and sipping mauby from a chipped enamel cup. Beside her, Devi's father sat cross legged on a low stool, mending a fishing net and listening to an old Bollywood song playing from the radio.

He looked up when he saw me, eyes squinting, not unkind, just measuring.

“This is my friend.”

Her father’s lips twitched, almost a smile.

“Friend, is it? Welcome. You hungry?”

I shook my head. No never felt like enough in front of people like that, people who made you feel welcome just by being still.

Her mother nodded politely, glanced at Devi, and asked if I was from Franklin Town.

Devi answered before I could. Her voice had that light sharpness daughters use when they don’t want their mothers reading too deep.

We stayed only ten minutes, maybe less. Just enough time for me to feel the heat of the lantern on my skin, to hear someone inside saying evening prayers in Hindi, while another child whistled the chorus to a calypso song.

Before we left, her mother pressed two roti into my hand, wrapped in wax paper.

“Eat it later. You look like you work hard.”

On the walk back, I had a lot of thoughts running through my head. Thinking about how love could grow in a place with two gods and five children and one crooked gate. About how her family didn't match but fit.

And for the first time, I started to wonder if the problem wasn't that our house was too strict but that it was too small to hold more than one way of being.

Three weeks passed. My routine was pretty much work, cookshop, and tease Kamla.

Finally my teasing came to an end.

The letter came folded in gold trimmed paper, sealed with saffron wax and a neat line of Sanskrit at the top. Ma read it three times before saying a word, her mouth moving silently like she was praying with her eyes. Kamla said nothing at first. Just sipped her tea and tapped her fingers against the glass, her face unreadable.

The boy's family was from Mandeville, respectable people, temple going, sugar merchants with land, they said. His name was Arvind. Twenty six. Studied accounting. Quiet, proper, not a drinker, the letter boasted. And when Ma read that out loud, Shanti muttered, "He sound boring already."

They agreed to meet on a Sunday afternoon. The house was scrubbed til the floor gleamed. Fresh flowers picked. Papa wore his good white kurta. Kamla's hair was oiled and braided with jasmine, sari pleats tucked sharp like paper edges. She didn't say a word, not even to me, and that silence was louder than the front gate when it creaked open.

Arvind stepped into the yard behind his parents, tall, dark skinned, with thick eyebrows and hands too big for someone so soft spoken. He bowed to Ma, shook Ba's hand with both of his, and gave Kamla one glance that said nothing and everything at once.

The families sat facing each other like it was business. Tea was poured. Biscuits passed. Auntie and Miss Shirley from next door peeked through the louvres. I sat on the steps with Percy, watching the way Kamla fingers tightened on her cup every time someone mentioned "settling down." She smiled when expected, nodded when polite, but her eyes never landed on Arvind's for more than a minute.

After pleasantries, Arvind was asked to walk our modest yard with Kamla. Mama pretended not to listen. Ba sipped whatever was in his cup in silence. I stood near the mango tree, pretending to look busy, when I caught them talking—

soft, stiff words about the weather, books, and the price of rice.

He didn't touch her. He didn't charm her. But he was gentle. And I watched her shoulders relax, just slightly, as if she was allowing herself to try.

When they came back, she said simply, "He's alright."

And in a house where arranged marriage was stitched in the curtains, that was more than enough.

After the commotion, I found her on the back steps, sari folded up to her knees, her feet resting in the cold grass. She had let her braid loose and was picking at the ends like she used to do when we were children and she was nervous before a school test. The house was quiet behind us, Mama's snores floating through the wood slats, the kitchen still holding the scent of clove and fried flour.

"You alright?"

She didn't look at me right away. Just nodded, then shook her head.

"It feel strange… knowing who I am supposed to marry. Knowing his name before I know his mind."

I sat beside her pulling my knees up. Crickets chirped loud in the bush, like they were trying to fill the silence between us.

"He's kind. Gentle. Smells like ink and soap. But I don't feel anything, you know? Not a flutter. Not like how the temple songs talk about love?"

"Maybe it will come later?"

She looked at me then, eyes narrow like she was studying a map on my face.

"Do you really think so Pops? Or you just saying that so I don't fall apart?"

"I believe some people find love before marriage. Some find it after. And some just never do."

She exhaled slowly.

"Do you think I am wrong? For not chasing something more?"

I took a moment before answering.

"I think you are braver than me. You are choosing peace. Stability. That is a kind of courage too. But don't lie to yourself just to make everyone else comfortable. Not even Mama."

She nodded again, slower this time. Then leaned her head on my shoulder like she used to when we were little and the thunder got too loud.

“Pops, if I do this, promise me you will always remind me of who I was. Just in case I forget.”

“Always.”

And we sat there, in the dark of our family’s yard, with the past behind us and the future pressing in, neither of us sure if we were running toward it or away.

The weeks before the engagement prep started, I found Raj out by the shed, rolling a cigarette with the patience of a priest. He didn’t smoke much these days, not since the coughing started. But tonight, he lit up slow, dragged in deep, and looked at me like he already knew what I was coming to say.

“She really going through with it.”

He exhaled without answering. The smoke curled upward, disappearing like names in the dust.

“You remember how Riya used to laugh?”

That got him. His jaw shifted. He nodded once.

"Now she only sends letters talking about blood pressure, how many pills she have to sort out for the man mother, and how much water to boil for foot soak."

"She does her duty," Raj responded.

"Yeah, but at what price?"

The words hung between us, thick as the Kingston heat. I leaned against the wall, arms folded tight.

"I just don't want Kamla to vanish like that. I know she says she fine, but I see the way her smile don't reach her eyes no more. Like she already packing away pieces of herself to fit into a man's house."

Raj didn't respond right away. He just looked out at the yard, where the breadfruit tree cast shadows like old secrets.

"Pops, you cya save people from tradition, bwoy. Especially when they choose it. Only thing you can do is love them loud enough so they don't forget who they were before it."

I didn't say anything. I just nodded, heart knotted up tight in my chest. And then we heard her voice.

Riya.

Calling from the front gate. She was early.

She stepped into the yard with a soft hello, carrying bags of fabric and sweets, wrapped in a sari the color of burnt rose. Thinner than I remembered. Quieter too. Her face wore a smile, but it looked borrowed.

Kamla came rushing out to greet her, and they embraced with a kind of force that almost cracked the stillness of the night. Shanti came too, all laughter and commentary. Even Ba stepped outside. Ma's voice called out from the kitchen, already handing out instructions.

The house came alive again.

But me? I just watched.

My sister was home, but not fully.

And Kamla was on her way out.

And I stood between them, one sister already given, one sister about to go, and all I could think was:

What will be left of us when the women we love start disappearing into other people's houses?

CHAPTER 6: TALK DONE. RING COME

The house moved like a pot about to boil over. From the front room to the backyard, it was all hands on deck. Shanti was hanging marigold garlands over the veranda rails, scolding Percy for stepping on the clean sheet Mama laid down to dry. Amara was oiling Kamla's hair on a stool near the back door, while Riya supervised with the quiet efficiency of a woman who had been through this dance already. Her face unreadable, her tone sweet but edged. Even Raj, usually so still, was tying bundles of rice and turmeric in muslin, his thick fingers surprisingly gentle. Ba and Anil were tending to the animals. We needed the best goat and chicken for the feast that was to come.

Kamla's engagement had turned the house into a village. Aunties from Clarendon came in with mango chutney packed in glass jars wrapped in rags. Cousins from Montego Bay showed up with stories, suitcases, and enough opinion to choke a goat. Even Mama's cousin Radhika arrived in a puff of lavender and judgment.

Later that evening, I noticed Kamla sitting near the front window, like a bride in training. Wrapped in fresh cotton, arms crossed, letting the aunties fuss with her hair and jewelry. She wore a smile like a pressed flower. Perfect, delicate, but already a little faded. Mama floated from room to room in her long skirt, fitted shirt, and tied head, barking orders in Hindi and patois in equal measure, forehead glistening with purpose.

Everyone had a role, and she was the enforcer.

And me? I slipped out the back gate while nobody was looking.

The lane outside was warm and humming. I did not even take the main road. I cut across the cane path and caught a passing bus to Papine, leaning against the window, watching the hills fold and unfold like the inside of a letter never sent.

She was at the restaurant, as I hoped. Sweeping the front, forehead damp, lips slightly chapped. She did not look surprised to see me. Just gave me that half smile that always knocked the words out of my mouth.

"Shouldn't you be at a wedding meeting?" she asked.

"They are planning love. Me a live it."

She rolled her eyes, but did not send me away. Instead she moved to the side, letting me sit on the bench near the door where the scent of cardamom floated just enough to remind me of home, but not enough to pull me back.

We did not talk much that day. Just sat. Her hand brushed mine once when she passed me a glass of water, and for a moment I thought, maybe this is enough. This quiet. This small defiance.

Back home I am sure they were rolling dough and rolling out promises. But in Papine under the rustling ackee tree, I was learning how love does not always arrive with fanfare. Sometimes it just sits beside you, barefoot and breathing.

Kamla noticed he was gone before anyone else did.

It was not that the house fell apart without him. The cousins still gossiped, the chutney still boiled, the decorations still twisted into shape. But something was missing in the noise. Like a missing note in a song only she could hear.

She saw it in the way Percy stopped mid sentence during a joke, glancing toward the back door. She saw it in Mama's momentary pause between barked instructions, eyes scanning the crowd for a son she had assumed was just in the yard. But it was Kamla who knew where he had gone.

Of course he had gone to Papine.

Her hands were dipped in turmeric paste, but her mind was already on her brother's lopsided smile, the way he bit the inside of his cheek when he was caught lying about where he had been. She imagined him sitting on that bench outside the little cookshop with the girl, the one with the steady eyes and cinnamon skin, the one who made him quieter and gentler.

She did not blame him. Not really.
She just wished she had done the same before it was too late.

Kamla turned back to the work in front of her, folding marigold petals into small cones for the ceremony, and sighed. Not from exhaustion, but from a grief that had not yet found its name. The kind of grief you feel when someone you love is walking away from your world, not because they do not love you, but because they have found something worth walking toward.

And in that moment, she did not feel like a bride.
She felt like a sister, watching her brother choose love over tradition, and wondering if she would ever have the chance to do the same.

The house had gone still by the time I came back. The cousins were tucked in wherever they could fit in our ever expanding house, mattresses pulled to corners, bodies sprawled across chairs, the smell of coconut oil and curry leaf still clinging to the air. Even Mama had finally let herself rest, her slippers halfway off, the last prayer half mumbled on her lips.

I moved quietly, thinking I could sneak in without stirring anything.

But there she was.

Kamla.

Sitting alone at the kitchen table, sari blouse loosened, hair down, a half finished plate of sweet rice in front of her, the spoon untouched.

She did not look up right away.
"Papine was nice?"

I froze. Then let out a breath I did not know I was holding and pulled out the chair across from her.
"Mi only gone for a few hours."

"That is all it takes, eh? A few hours fi feel like freedom?" she replied.

She was not teasing, not fully. But her eyes were not hard either. Just tired. Soft.

"Yuh vex Kam?"

"No Pops, I envy you."

We sat there, silent for a while, the kitchen clock ticking loud in the quiet. A stray dog barked in the lane. The ceiling fan clicked with each turn.

"I see the way yuh look when you leaving here to go see her. Or the way yuh look when you reach in from there. Like yuh finally get fi breathe."

"Kam yuh coulda wait too."

She shook her head slowly.
"Some of us too deep in it already. Yuh brave. Me? I just trying not to disappoint anybody."

I reached for her hand, calloused from days of prep, stained with turmeric, still warm.
I looked at her. "If you ever need to remember who you are before all this, I will remind yuh. Every time."

She smiled then. For real this time.
"Same for you Pops. Do not let Mama pick yuh bride. Yuh hear me?"

"Me nuh plan to."

And just like when we were children, we sat in the kitchen long after midnight, two siblings trying to hold onto each other while the world around us kept folding and unfolding like freshly pressed saris before the big day.

Suddenly my ears perked up.

Raj Jr came walking in with his shoes in his hand.

I raised my eyebrows. First, I thought my big brother was in his bed, probably babysitting Anil since the cousins took over his. Second, I could tell he thought he could sneak in, hence the shoes in hand.

"Is where yuh a come from," I said.

This was the last person I expected to see sneaking out.
Raj, the top a top pikney.

"Just did a walk pon the lane and check Jerome," he said, not making our eyes connect.

Kamla eyed him suspiciously and smirked.
"Sure Raj. Sure. Member say is woman me name. Women mind run deeper than man river."

"And sometime it run too deep fi yuh own good," Raj responded defensively.

He walked off to his bedroom without giving her enough time for a comeback.

I was too caught up in my own love story to notice Raj's behavior.

"He has been moving different," Kam said.

Not loud. Not rebellious like me. Just off rhythm. Quiet in a way that was not natural. Not the usual silence he carried like a shawl, but something heavier. He would disappear for hours under the excuse of errands or helping out Jerome or another friend.

Even during the engagement prep, while Mama barked and Kamla sighed, Raj just nodded, smiled when expected, and kept his mouth shut.
And I was too caught up to notice how big of a change it was.

I was putting the pieces neat together now like a puzzle. Shanti squinted at him the other night at dinner, watching how he stirred his food but barely ate it. Ba asked him something about fixing the shed, and he stared off like he did not even hear. But it was Kamla who caught it best. At dinner earlier in the week she said,

"Yuh ever notice how Raj always leave right before sunset now?"

Of course I would not notice. I was never home. But the rest of the family had.
Maybe Raj had found his own secret, worth holding onto. And if he had, I was not sure I wanted to take part in exposing it.

It was past midnight when Raj knocked on my door.
He never knocked. Usually he just came in, nodded, passed a joke, or we sat in a comfortable silence if the mood was right. But this time, there was a knock, soft but deliberate.

I opened the door, expecting a chore, a warning, maybe a complaint from the General of York Street. But he just stood there in the shadows, arms crossed, face unreadable.
"Come walk with mi Pops."

We did not speak for a while. Just walked. Past the tamarind tree. Past the rusted gate that creaked like old gossip. Past the bush Mama said not to touch after dark.
Then, as if the weight finally tipped over, he said it.
"I meet someone."

I turned.
"Wha yuh mean, meet someone? Like… meet or meet?"

He gave a tight smile.
"Black girl. Name Charmaine. She teach little ones at the church school up near Allman Town. Protestant."

Those words hung in the air like thunder before rain.
Black. Then Protestant.
I did not know whether to laugh or choke.

"You serious?"

He nodded, eyes steady.
"Met her when I went to collect some roofing boards for Uncle Dataram. She was there with a Bible, talking to two boys fighting over a cricket bat. She split them up faster than Mama splits coconut. And she laugh. Mi God, she laugh like sugar drop in lime tea. Sweet, and sharp."

I stared at him. My perfect quiet, first born male heir. The one who kept his shirt tucked, his thoughts folded.
"Yuh love her?" I asked.

He did not answer right away.
"Mi do not know what love feel like. But when I don't see her, mi chest feel like rope twist up. And when I do, the whole world feel softer."

We kept walking. The breeze warm. The moon peeking out from behind clouds like it was listening.

"Mama nah approve. Ba nuh watch nuh face, breeze still blow his way. But you know the old lady." He stopped.
"I know. That's why mi keep it hush."

"And after?" I asked.

"After Kamla marry. After things settle. Maybe then. Maybe I ask her to meet the family. Maybe I finally stop living safe and start living true."

I looked at him then, not as my older brother, not as the example Mama always held us to, but as a man trying to hold onto something fragile. Something beautiful.
And I realized we were both in love. Just with different type of impossible.

The first time Raj truly relaxed was under the almond tree outside Charmaine's classroom. He had taken off his shoes. His sleeves were rolled up. He leaned back against the thick trunk like it knew his secrets. And Charmaine was beside him—barefoot, chalk dust on her skirt, her hair wrapped in a bright a red scarf that caught the afternoon like fire.

She laughed at something he said—loud, full bodies, unafraid. Not like the way women laugh around Mama. Not like the way Kamla's future mother-in-law measures each smile like salt in a stew. Charmaine laughed like nobody was watching.

And Raj…he laughed too. Really laughed. His head tilted back, teeth showing, shoulders shaking. The kind of laugh that lives in your belly for days.

"You always so quiet around people?" Charmaine asked.

"Only when I don't trust them."

She raised an eyebrow , teasing.

"And me?" She asked.

He glanced at her, then looked away like the sun was too bright.

"You feel like something I should've known long time ago."

She didn't answer. Just reached out, traced a finger along the scar on his hand—the one he got fixing the gate when we were boys. He flinched slightly , but didn't pull away.

"Your family ever meet someone like me?"

He hesitated. Then told the truth.

"Yes. As friends."

They sat like that, beneath the tree, surrounded by the hum of insects and far off music drifting from someone's backyard. The scent of curry leaf, the sound of breeze through dry grass, the warmth of a woman who didn't pray to his god—but held him like she'd been sent anyway.

And in that moment, Raj wasn't a son, or a brother, or a man with a secret.

He was simply a man…falling in love with freedom.

Later that night, the family convened for the engagement of the year.

The drums started long before the guests arrived.
From the back of the yard, the dhol echoed against the zinc fencing, vibrating through the coconut trees like a heartbeat. Aunties bustled in every direction, adjusting garlands, scattering rose petals, shooing flies off trays of ladoo and jalebi. Cousins tied sashes, powdered cheeks, pinned jasmine into freshly oiled hair.

The yard was transformed.
Our little two room house that expanded into seven rooms over the years had turned into paradise. Banana leaves hung from the gate, strings of marigold swayed from the veranda,

and the scent of curry, clove, and sandalwood wrapped itself around everyone like incense. Plates clinked, children laughed, uncles shouted over each other with false wisdom and rum on their breath.

And in the middle of it all, Kamla sat like a carved goddess, wrapped in red and gold, bangles to her elbows, kajal lining her eyes just right. She did not smile often, but when she did, it came in flashes, like light on river water. Enough to remind you there was still life under the surface.

My old lady was glowing. Bossing. Praying. Crying. All at once.
Ba stood near the gate in his white kurta, nodding at each guest like a quiet king.
And me, I stood in the corner with a sweet drink in my hand, watching it all, watching my sister take the first step into someone else's life.

The groom's family arrived with fanfare, gifts in baskets, silk scarves folded just so, and too much perfume. Arvind was polite, steady, respectful. He bowed to the elders, smiled at the cousins, took Kamla's hand with practiced grace. The aunties sighed. Mama nodded. Ba gave his rare approval with a tight smile and a pat on the back.

But I saw my sister's fingers twitch.
Just once.
Enough to remind me that even the steadiest of hands can tremble.

Raj stood beside Ba, arms folded, expression unreadable. But I caught the way his eyes wandered toward the gate, like he expected someone else to walk in. Someone darker.
Someone Protestant.

As the priest began the blessings, Kamla glanced up at me.
Just for a second.
It was not a look of fear or regret.
It was something else. A silent message passed between siblings in the middle of a sea of incense and approval.
"I am doing this. But do not forget who I am."
I nodded back.
"I never could."

The drums picked up again. The sweets were passed. The elders chanted. The ring was placed on her finger. And just like that, Kamla was promised.
The music roared, but underneath it, I could still hear something else.
A quiet shifting. A kind of goodbye.

Chapter 6: Talk Done, Ring Come

The house smelled like leftovers and incense.

It was late, long after the guests had left, after the drums stopped, after the laughter softened into yawns and whispers. Ma had gone to bed humming a bhajan under her breath, Ba had nodded off with his slippers still on, and the cousins were strewn across couches and corners like forgotten decorations.

Me, Kamla, and Raj were in the yard, cleaning what was left of the celebration. Paper lanterns dropping, empty glasses rattling in a crate, the scent of cardamom tea still clinging to the veranda.

Kamla, barefoot and finally free of her jewelry, was stacking plates when she paused.

"So Raj…where you sneak off to before the ring ceremony?"

I froze mid sweep.

"Mi never sneak off," Raj replied. He did not even look up. Just kept folding tablecloths.

"Yuh sure? Cause the old lady call yuh name twice and yuh magically reappear just in time for the family photo."

She was teasing, but not really.

Raj looked at me. Then looked away.
I chimed in, “Man probably gone fi fresh air. All the incense could choke the goat them.”

Kamla squinted, stepping closer.
“Raj, yuh smelling like bay rum and something else. Not curry. Not incense. Something sweet. Like—”

“Yuh imagining things.”

That was when Percy, little Percy who should be sleeping but still sharp as a tack, popped up from behind the sheet Ma laid out to dry and said, loud as ever,
“Mi see Uncle Raj hug a lady outside Allman Town last week! She wear a bright sari and call him baby!”

Silence.
Everything froze. Even the crickets seemed to stop chirping.

“What?”
“Percy, hush,” I said.

But Raj did not deny it.
He just exhaled, deep and slow, then looked up at both of us with tired eyes.
“Her name is Charmaine.”

Kam's lips parted.

"Charmaine…is Indian?"

"No. She is black. And Protestant."

The words dropped like guava from a too ripe tree.

Kamla's hands dropped to her sides. My broom slipped from my grip.

Nobody said anything for a long while. Just the quiet, the night wrapping around us, tight and unblinking.

"Mama…would break."

Raj sighed deep, the kind that pulled from bone. Then he said, "Then she better start bending."

And with that, Raj walked past us, through the back door, into the house.

His secret no longer hidden. Just sitting there on the veranda with us, like an uninvited guest.

CHAPTER 7- THREE NAMES. THREE ROADS

If Kamla's wedding was a river in flood, noisy and restless, carrying the whole house along with it, then Devi was my still water. Calm, clear, the place where I could see my own reflection without breaking it into pieces. And I longed to take a dive.

I went to her that Tuesday afternoon, slipping away from the endless wedding chatter and Mama's sharp voice assigning everyone a chore. The yard was full of Arvind's relatives, voices spilling over each other like they had come to buy out the whole island. Inside, the smell of turmeric, cardamom, and something frying made the walls sweat. I could barely breathe.

But the moment I stepped into Barrington's shop in Papine, the noise fell away. She was behind the counter, hair tied back, a red scarf knotted at her neck, weighing lentils for an old woman who called her "child" with a smile. She looked up, caught my eye, and there it was—that quiet, unspoken welcome. No words. Just a peace that found its way into my bones.

We walked later, up past the cricket field where the boys were batting with a bent stick, through the side street where the smell of fresh roti drifted from an open window. She did not ask about the wedding. I did not have to tell her about the mountains of marigold and the loud-mouthed uncles. Instead, we talked about Kingston at night, the music from Halfway Tree, and the way the air changed before the rain.

But even as I laughed with her, Raj's face kept flickering in my mind, how he looked the day before, how his voice carried both fear and freedom when he described Charmaine to me again. At home, Kamla was fitting her wedding sari, practicing her smile in the mirror, pretending not to be nervous. Arvind's name was on every tongue. In another part of Kingston, Raj was holding Charmaine's hand. And here I was, with Devi, wondering which road my own feet would take, and how long I could keep Ma from trying to pave it for me.

"So tell mi now, yuh ever been in love before?" Devi asked me.
"Why? Yuh planning fi write a book bout mi?" I asked.
"Mi just asking a simple question. Nuh swell yuh head."

"Alright, once. Thought it was love. Turn out she love mi cricket bat and mi bicycle."

"Lawd, so she bruk yuh heart?"

"Nah man, mi still deh yah. But mi learn quick, don't give away yuh bat."

She rested her chin in her palm, eyes shining like she was storing away every word.

"Mi memba when mi likkle, mi fada tell mi love is like curry. Must season proper before yuh cook it, else it cyan taste good."

"So wha seasoning yuh use?"

"Patience, kindness, and likkle pepper fi keep it fun."

"So yuh telling me fi be patient, kind, and peppery?"

"After all that, mi nuh tell yuh nothing. Mi just a talk bout curry," she responded cheekily.

We both laughed, but something warm settled between us, an understanding that we were already stirring our own pot, slow and careful, just the way her father would have approved.

"Alright, since yuh love ask question but nuh answer them straight, mi want hear one story bout yuh as a boy."

"One story? Woman, mi have whole heap."

"Just one good one. Something mek mi laugh and know who yuh really is."

I leaned back, smiling at the memory that bubbled up.
"I was nine. Ba buy mi a likkle goat. Mi call him Bullet, cause him did bold, nuh fraid a nobody. Mi used to tie him up inna the front yard and sometime mi never memba fi tie the rope tight. Ba used to cuss mi bout it, til one day, Bullet buss rope an run straight down to cricket field while mi team a bat. Goat tek the ball in him mouth an run all round town like him scoring six. Whole match done, everybody laugh. Mi did want move mi bed to the field cause mi kno Mama and Ba did have a cussing for mi."

She turned to me laughing. "Lawd yuh grow up trouble from long time!"
"An yuh still here talking to mi, so yuh must like trouble."
"Maybe."

For a moment, we just looked at each other, the street noise fading, the smell of spice and roasted corn in the air. The story was just a story, but the way she held my gaze made it feel like she had been part of it all along.

It was early morning, the kind of quiet that only existed before Ma started her chanting and the crows began their useless debate in the breadfruit tree.

I was on the veranda sipping bush tea, watching dew bead along the hibiscus leaves, when Raj stepped out. No shoes, no words, just that same tension he had been carrying like an old satchel since Kam's engagement. He stood there for a while, arms crossed, looking out at the street like he expected instructions.

"Yuh tell her yet?" I asked.
He didn't ask who.
"No."
"Yuh plan to?"

That's when he sat. Not like he wanted to rest, but like he couldn't stand any longer.
"I am going to marry her."

I blinked. Thought maybe I misheard.
"Yuh mean talk to Ma and Ba, explain it—"
"No," he said.

"You serious?" I asked.
"Mi too old to wait on permission to live. If I wait, they going to find a girl with the right last name, the right dowry,

the right shade of brown, and mi going to wake up ten years from now with three pickney and a house full of silence." He paused. "With her, I laugh. I feel light. Mi feel like more than just the eldest son carrying tradition on my back like a bag of yam."

I looked at him—really looked at him. The lines around his eyes, the way his hands never rested, always fidgeting now. The man who once walked like he was born with a map in his hand was now walking off the page.

"Yuh know what this go mean, right? Mama…she not just going to cry. She going mourn you like yuh dead."
He nodded, eyes distant.
"So be it. Let her mourn who she think I was. Mi still love her. But mi done trying to be her dream."

I didn't have anything clever to say. Just sat there beside him, listening to the far-off rooster, the rustling ackee leaves, the sound of a man deciding to free himself no matter the cost.
"So when?" I asked.
"This week. Quietly. Just we and the pastor."
I nodded, chest tight.
"Yuh sure?"
"First time ever in my life."

A Quiet Wednesday in Allman Town…

The church was small, whitewashed, and plain. No stained glass, no altar bells, just wooden pews, a cloth-covered pulpit, and the scent of polished floors and old hymnals. The kind of place where faith was humble and love did not need decoration to be real.

Raj stood in the second row, straight-backed, palms sweaty. He wore a cream button-down shirt tucked into his best trousers, creased, ironed, stiff with care. No one from home knew. No one had been invited. Except me.

Charmaine entered through the side door with a smile that could part clouds. Her hair was wrapped in yellow this time, the color of ripe June mangoes. Her dress was soft and simple, cotton with lace at the sleeves, and she carried no flowers. She walked herself down the aisle. Raj could not look away.

The pastor, a stout woman with salt and pepper hair and the voice of a Sunday breeze, spoke gentle and clear.
"Marriage is not a ceremony. It is a choice made daily. To stand with one another. In sun. In storm."

There were only six people in the room. Me. Two of Charmaine's friends. Her uncle. The pastor. And God. But it was enough.

They said their vows quietly, like they were promises whispered under a sheet, like they knew the world outside would not approve and so they did not give it the privilege of hearing.

"I promise to honor your fire, to hold your joy, and to build a life with you, even if we have to build it with our bare hands," I heard my brother say.

"I promise to love all of you. Not just what you show, but what you hide. Even if your family never knows my name, I will still carry yours with pride."

And just like that, it was done. No rice thrown. No drums. No marigolds. Just love. Quiet. Real.

After the blessing, Raj stepped outside, took Charmaine's hand, and for the first time kissed her like a man who had nothing left to lose and everything to gain.

We did not take pictures. But I will remember it forever. Because that was the day my brother became his own man. Not the golden boy. Not the first-born son of Ba. Just Raj. And he was finally free.

For a week, Raj was everywhere and nowhere at once. He left the house early, before Ba's first cup of tea, and returned after the lamps were lit. When Ma asked where he had been, he would smile, shrug, and change the subject to Kam's wedding sari or whether the goat pen needed fixing. I could see the truth in his eyes, but I kept my mouth shut.

Charmaine's scent, rosewater and talc, lingered faintly on his shirts. He tried to wash them himself, scrubbing at the standpipe in the yard, but Ma caught a whiff once and frowned. "What you doing with perfume pon yuh collar?" she asked. Raj just laughed and said the tailor wore too much.

Inside the house, the noise of Kamla's wedding preparations masked almost everything. Aunty Prem's bangles clinked as she rolled dough in the kitchen. Ba and two uncles argued over how many tables the yard could hold. Every doorway seemed to have a cousin standing in it, watching the bustle like they were at a play.

It was the perfect cover for Raj. The family's eyes were elsewhere. No one thought to wonder why he had become such an expert at vanishing.

At night, when the house settled and the only light was the peenie wallies and the only sound was the crickets, I would lie on the veranda thinking about it all. Raj's wedding. Kam's wedding. And the beautiful girl waiting for me in Papine. I wondered how long Raj's freedom would last before someone pulled the curtain back.

He never asked me to keep his secret, and I never promised to. But he knew. And I knew. And sometimes, when he caught my eye across the dinner table, there was a silent thank you in his eyes.

It was late afternoon when the postman rattled the gate and handed Anil a small stack of envelopes. Most were the usual, an uncle in Mandeville sending his blessings for the wedding, a bill from the tailor. But one was different. Thick cream paper, the address in a careful hand.

The old lady did not think twice before sliding her finger under the flap. Inside, on official registrar paperwork, were the words:

Certificate of Marriage. Raj Singh Jr. and Charmaine Edwards.

Her eyes froze on the line, the paper trembling just slightly in her hand. She read it twice, three times, the name

Charmaine looking as out of place in our family as a sorrel plant blooming in the snow.

I was at the table fixing the brass lamps for the wedding tomorrow when she called me.
"Come here boy."

Her voice was not sharp, but it was the kind that made your stomach tighten. She held the letter out without a word. I read it quickly, my heart kicking hard in my chest.

"You knew," she said quietly. Not a question. An accusation dressed as fact.

I swallowed. "Ma, is not my story to tell."

She drew herself up, straightening her sari pleats, the hurt in her eyes burning hotter than any anger. "This is how I find out? From a piece of paper from the government? Not from him?"

Before I could answer, the front door banged open. Raj came in, smiling like the sun had been following him all day. Then he saw the letter in Ma's hand, the air in the room turning heavy enough to choke on.

"Is this true?"

His smile faded, but his eyes did not drop. “Yes. I am married to a girl name Charmaine.”

The room stayed silent for a long, hot minute. Outside, someone in the yard was laughing, not knowing that inside our house, something had just shifted forever.

Mama’s breath came slow and heavy, as though each one had to fight its way past her heart. She set the letter on the table like it burned her fingers. “Mi raise yuh with all the customs, all the respect, all the ways of my people, and this is wa yuh do?”

Raj stepped closer, voice low but steady. “Mama, mi love her.”

“If it was right, yuh would not keep it secret Raj.” She shot back, her bangles clinking, her tie head unraveling. She turned her face away, but not before I saw the wetness in her eyes.

Ba had been standing in the doorway the whole time, his shadow stretching into the room. He did not speak right away. Ba never rushed words. He walked to the table, picked up the letter, and read it slowly. Then he looked at Raj, not with anger, but with a deep, tired disappointment.

"Marriage is not just love, Raj," he said at last. "It is roots. It is the blood that carry on the name. But you already done it now, so my only hope is that you treat her good. You are still our son."

That was all. Ba left the room, his slippered feet soft against the tile. The weight of his words was heavier than Mama's shouting.

The quiet did not last. Auntie Prem, always hovering near the kitchen, had heard enough to stitch the story together. By the time the sun slipped behind the breadfruit tree, every cousin, every aunt, and every neighbor leaning over the fence knew. Raj had married in secret. The rest, they would learn later.

Some whispered, some cursed under their breath, and some smiled like they saw no shame in it. Kamla, sitting in her wedding sari for final fittings, stared at the wall with wide eyes. "So not just my wedding we a talk now."

CHAPTER 8 WHEN THE YARD EMPTY

Mama's voice carried through the whole house now.
"So you not only hide from me, you shame me in front of the whole family? Raj, you know well it is the wife who come live with the husband family. That is how we keep the roots strong, that is how we raise the children together, under one roof, one tradition."

Her bangles clattered against each other as she paced, sari pleats swaying sharply with each step. She was not just angry. She was wounded. In her mind, every child's marriage was another stitch in the fabric of the family, and Raj had cut his own thread without her blessing.

Raj stood still, leaning against the wall like he was trying to keep his footing in a storm.
"Mama. I do not know if bringing Charmaine here is the best. She different. She did not grow with the same customs. I do not want her to feel like a stranger in her own house."

"This is not her house yet," she snapped.
"It is your house. Your father's house. Your brothers' house. Women learn. They adjust."

He rubbed his forehead, sighing.
“Maybe I do not want her to have to adjust. Maybe I want her to be free.”

From the corner, I could see our older brother’s eyes darting between them. He knew the rule as well as any of us. Sons brought their wives home, and the whole family shared the same roof. That was the tradition, the shield, the way we survived.

But Raj was not sure. Not because he did not love us, but because he knew Charmaine might not survive the weight of Mama’s sharp tongue and strict ways. And maybe, deep down, he did not want to risk watching the two women he loved most pulling each other apart.

Eventually, after the initial shock and yelling the letter caused, the family was forced to face that Raj was married. Mama fumed, Ba went quiet. And Kam muttered that her brother had stolen attention from her wedding. But no one knew who Charmaine really was. Raj kept it vague, saying things like, “She good, she kind, she can cook,” but leaving out the truth.

Some of the cousins whispered. Why no proper introduction? Why no family blessing? Why no visit from the bride? But with Kamla's wedding preparations consuming the house, the matter drifted into the background.

Later that night, Auntie Prem said, "Mi nuh hear the girl family name yet. Which village she come from?"
Raj just smiled and said, "She come from town side."

That was enough to quiet some, but not Mama. She watched him close, her instincts sharper than anyone else's. She knew there was more he was not saying.

For me, it was torture to hold the truth. I felt torn. Torn to protect Raj or to prepare Mama for the bigger shock still to come. Meanwhile, the house was full of Kamla's bangles clinking, sari fabric laid out on the bed, uncles building a tent frame in the yard. No one noticed Raj slipping out at odd hours. No one except Mama.

Wedding Day

The house woke before dawn. Aunties clattered in the kitchen, pots steaming with dhal, curry goat, chicken, pumpkin. Uncles argued over chairs in the yard, moving them this way and that. Kamla sat in the corner room with Mama, Rose, Shanti, Amara, and cousins. Bangles stacked to her elbows, eyes downcast as the final touches were made.

But beneath all the noise and the smell of spices, the air was tight. Everyone's smile stretched a little too thin. The letter from yesterday still hung over the house like smoke after a fire. Raj moved quietly, avoiding Mama's eyes. Nobody spoke Charmaine's name, but I knew everyone was thinking it.

In the middle of it all, I slipped outside to the veranda where the morning sun was painting the yard gold. My nephew came running up, quick footed, bright eyes, a piece of fried dumpling still in his hand.

"Uncle Pops, mi ready fi di work today!" he said, grinning.

I pulled a folded paper from my pocket and lowered my voice.
"This one not for the wedding. Is a different kind of work."

He took the note eagerly, puffing his chest out like a soldier. "Fi who, Uncle?"

"For Devi. You know the restaurant? Slip it to her hand. Nobody else. Tell her after all this wedding done, I want to carry her out. Just me and her."

The boy's eyes lit with mischief. "So mi a postman now?"

"Best one in Kingston," I said, giving him a pat on his head. "And keep it quiet, hear?"

By midday, the yard was full. Relatives from Franklin Town, Mona, Vineyard Town, country, all gathered in their bright saris and starched kurtas. Drums beat slow and steady, calling the neighbors to the fence. Kamla stepped out, shining, even though her eyes stayed soft and distant. Arvind's people arrived in a small procession, bringing gifts and garlands.

The chanting began, the sacred fire was lit, and the marriage of Kamla and Arvind was sealed. My mother's face glowed with pride, Ba's with quiet relief. But my eyes kept drifting beyond the yard, towards Papine, where I knew my letter was in safe hands.

A few hours earlier at the cookshop...

The restaurant in Papine buzzed with the midday crowd. Truck drivers wiped sweat from their brows, women bargained for curry and roti to carry home. Devi moved among them with practiced grace, balancing trays, her dupatta tied neatly over her shoulder, the smell of dhal clinging to her hands.

That was when my nephew slipped in, dodging between the stools like a small mongoose. He climbed onto a chair, grinning wide.
"Miss Devi…my uncle send this," he whispered, sliding the folded paper into her palm like it was treasure. Then he winked and scampered out before she could scold him.

She looked down, her fingers trembling just slightly as she opened the note.

"*Today my sister gives her hand to another. Tomorrow, I want to ask for only your time. After all the smoke and singing fade, will you let me take you out, just us, to talk and laugh in peace? From the one who danced with you.*"

She pressed her lips together, fighting a smile. Her brother Rohan, wiping a counter nearby, caught the sparkle in her eyes.
"What dat? Who write yuh so?"

"Nutting," she said quickly, folding the paper and tucking it under her apron. But the blush on her cheeks betrayed her.

As she carried the next tray out to the tables, her steps were lighter. Her heart faster. She did not know exactly what tomorrow would bring, but the thought of it made the whole busy restaurant feel brighter.

Back at Franklin Town

By evening, the yard glowed with lanterns strung between mango trees. Plates clattered, the smell of curry goat, roti, and sweet gulab jamun floated through the air. Men slapped dominoes at the far table, women sang folk songs in Hindi and Bhojpuri, and children darted underfoot with sticky hands.

The drums grew louder as the dhol players from Clarendon arrived, beating out rhythms that pulled everyone to their feet. Kamla and her new husband were coaxed into the center, their shy smiles breaking into laughter as cousins circled them, clapping and singing. But beneath the glitter and cheer, I could feel the tension buzzing like a mosquito in the night. Every so often, Mama's eye flickered toward Raj, sharp and suspicious. He smiled politely, but his gaze kept drifting toward the gate, as if waiting for someone.

In the middle of a song, while the drums drowned out footsteps, Raj eased toward the back of the yard. I caught him as he passed, his hand brushing my shoulder.
"Mi nah stay long," he whispered. "Mi just waan her see…just a likkle taste of the music."

I didn't need to ask who. I just nodded, though my stomach tightened. If Mama caught sight, the night would end in fire.

A few minutes later, I spotted them in the shadows by the gate. Charmaine stood just beyond the lantern light, her hand resting lightly in Raj's. She wore a simple dress, nothing like the saris swirling in 1¼ York Street, but her presence glowed. Her eyes widened as she watched the dancers, the colors, the laughter.

Raj bent close to her, whispering something that made her laugh softly. For a moment, I saw the ease in him I hadn't seen for weeks—the joy of a man finally standing with his heart in the open, even if only at the edge. But Mama was scanning the yard, and the drums would not cover his absence forever. I prayed he had the sense to slip her away before the wrong eyes noticed.

The yard was quiet the next day, only the scent of incense and stale curry lingering in the air. Stray flower petals stuck to the grass, chairs leaned against the wall, and the ashes of the sacred fire smoldered in the pit. Inside, Mama moved like a storm. Bangles clinking as she folded saris and scolded the cousins for not sweeping fast enough.

Kamla had gone with Arvind for the night, but she would be back later to pack the rest of her things and say her goodbyes. Her room already felt hollow. The whole house carried a strange emptiness, as though a string had been pulled loose.

But Raj was nowhere to be found.

At breakfast, Ba asked quietly, "Where him gone so early?" His voice wasn't sharp, but it made the table go still.
"Maybe with friends," one cousin muttered.
Mama narrowed her eye. "Friends, eh? Or di woman him too shame fi bring home?"

Her words hung heavy in the room. No one dared to answer. I kept my head down, stirring my porridge, though my mind raced. I knew where Raj had gone. And I knew the longer he stayed away, the closer Ma's suspicion would get to the truth.

He came back later in the afternoon, his shirt creased, his hair smelling of perfume, not his own. He tried to slip in quiet, but Ma was waiting on the veranda.
"Raj," she said, her voice low, dangerous. "Yuh not a bachelor boy now. Yuh married. Married man nuh disappear whole day after dem sister wedding. Where yuh gone?"

He hesitated, glancing at me, but said nothing. That silence was answer enough. Mama's mouth pressed thin, and Ba's eyes darkened, the air around the table thick again.

By the end of the next day, the house felt like it was unraveling. Kamla returned to gather her trunks—bright saris folded neatly, her jewelry cases, her books, and all the linens Mama had been sewing since she was a girl. She moved through her room slowly, fingers brushing against the wall as though trying to memorize it.

Mama hovered close, instructing her on what to pack, reminding her of all the duties waiting at her husband's family home. Kam smiled softly, nodding, though her eyes looked heavy. Ba stayed quiet on the veranda, eyes fixed on the ground. She hugged each of us in turn, whispering, "Don't forget me and tek care a one another, hear."

Just as her trunks were being carried out, Raj appeared. But he wasn't alone. At his side stood Charmaine, tall, poised, skin dark as tamarind bark. She smiled politely, nervous but proud, as Raj guided her up the path.

For a moment, the yard froze.

Mama's face darkened. "Raj…" Her voice cracked, sharp as a whip. "Is dis di woman yuh hide from we? A black gyal? A shame yuh shame me?"

Charmaine's smile faltered, but Raj lifted his chin. "This is my wife. She kind, she strong, and I love her. Me nuh shame."

Mama turned away, her bangles rattling. "Yuh betray yuh family. Ah better unu go back to weh yah come from."

Ba had been sitting in his chair by the doorway, silent, watching. At last he spoke, his voice deep but calm. "If this path yuh choose, Raj, den walk it. Yuh mother cyan stop yuh. Mi cyan stop yuh. But yuh cyan walk two road same time."

Raj's jaw clenched. He looked at Charmaine, then at us. His eyes softened for a moment, but his grip on her hand never loosened.

The silence was worse than shouting.

"Mi choose already," he said quietly.

He led her back through the gate, step by step, until they disappeared down the road.

No shouting, no curse, just the soft thud of footsteps fading away.

That night, the house was heavy with silence. Two beds were now empty, Kamala and Raj. Their laughter folded up and carried away. Mama sat stiff in her chair, eyes red but mouth hard as a stone. Ba smoked quietly on the veranda, staring out into the yard. Shanti and Anil occupied themselves with some books.

For the first time, the family felt smaller, not like a home overflowing with voices and laughter but like a shell where only echoes lived. Just three siblings remained, along with Mama and Ba.

The family that once seemed unbreakable had bent to the weight of love and tradition, and now it felt as though nothing could make it whole again. It was the first time I realized home could break, not with a single crack but piece by piece, until all that was left was silence.

CHAPTER 9 SINCE I MET YOU BABY

"Since I met you baby, my whole life has changed…" She sang along to the radio that afternoon in her yard, while I understood what she meant when she said her family was different.

I spent the whole day in Papine with her family. The house leaned against the hillside, its walls thin enough that you could hear laughter in one room and singing in another. Her father had strung prayer beads along the doorway, and in the corner of the sitting room stood a small brass murti of Lakshmi, polished bright. But when her mother lit the stove, her lips moved in quiet Arabic, whispering bismillah before dropping the roti on the tawa.

It wasn't a house divided, it was a house doubled. On one wall hung a framed verse from the Qur'an, on another a calendar with Lord Krishna dancing among the gopis. The children ran in and out, their bare feet dusty, their accents thick with yard slang. And nobody seemed to mind the mixture.

Her brothers Barry and Rohan clapped me on the back when I joined them, joking, "Man I don't know how yuh handle my sister soft ways, but yuh strong."

Her sisters giggled from the veranda, carrying trays of fried plantain and tamarind chutney, while Devi rolled her eyes and swatted them away.

For a while, I just sat and soaked it in, the clatter of pots, the scent of curry, the sound of two different prayers rising at different times of day yet never clashing. And in the middle of it all was Devi, moving between kitchen and table with a grace that reminded me of my mother but a freedom Mama had never allowed herself.

That evening, as I went home with the sound of their laughter still in my ears, I thought of Raj and Charmaine. He had chosen love, boldly, no matter the cost. And I realized I couldn't keep my own love tucked away in quiet corners of Kingston.

It was time. Time for Devi to meet my family, to walk through our gate, to sit at our table. Whether Mama welcomed her or not, I wanted her to know I was serious, that she was more than a secret dance, more than notes passed by my nephew.

I felt like I hadn't seen Raj in weeks. Not since he walked out the gate with Charmaine. The house had been hollow without him, no teasing in the evenings, no laughter spilling from his room, no whisper of his cricket bat thumping against the veranda rail. He hadn't even showed up to work in weeks.

That same evening, I decided to walk further down to Allman Town and seek out my big brother. I spotted him leaning against the fence by a big breadfruit tree. His shirt was rolled at the sleeves, his face tired but brighter somehow. Charmaine wasn't with him.

"Bwoy, yuh forget yuh have a brother?" I called out.

Raj's smile cracked wide, and for a second he looked just like the boy who used to drag me to watch cricket at Sabina.

"Mi nuh forget… yuh mad?"

We sat on the low stone wall, the dusk wrapping around us. He told me about Charmaine's laugh, about the little house they shared, about how people stared when they walked but he didn't care.

I admitted how empty the house felt without him, how Mama anger made the air tight, and Ba silence weighed heavier than words. He squeezed my shoulder and said, "Mi miss it too. But mi cyan live two life."

I nodded, throat tight. I did understand, maybe more than he knew. I had Devi in my thoughts every waking hour, and I couldn't imagine giving her up to keep tradition neat and tidy.

When we parted, he pulled me into a rough hug. "Mi hope when your time come, yuh brave enough," he whispered.

Walking home under the street lamps, I knew what I had to do next.

The next morning, I woke to the sound of chatter in the yard, voices overlapping like birds at dawn. When I came out to the veranda, the house was already alive.

Both my married sisters had dropped by, Kam and Riya, with their husbands, my troublesome nephew, and my sweet niece.

It was my father's birthday, and the table had been dressed with roti, pumpkin, saltfish, and a jug of sorrel for breakfast.

Mama hovered, making sure the oil lamps were lit just right, pressing trays into our hands, fussing as always. Ba sat tall in his chair, quieter than the noise around him, but I could see the pride in his eyes as he watched his children.

But one chair stayed empty, Raj's chair.

No one said his name, but we all felt it.

After breakfast, Mama's voice cut through the laughter. "So mi second son, when yuh going to stop play bachelor and let mi arrange a wife fi yuh?"

Ba grunted, half in agreement, half in jest. "Ah time, man. Cyan't work and play cricket forever."

All eyes turned to me. Percy was smirking, he knew too much.

I leaned back, met their stares, and shook my head. "No Mama. Mi nuh ready fi dat. Mi fine."

The table fell quiet for a moment, Mama frowning, Ba watching with that steady gaze. My sisters exchanged glances but said nothing. My little brother stayed silent and loyal.

I reached for my cup, trying to swallow the lump in my throat. I wasn't ready to tell them the truth, that my heart was already set, already given.

And definitely not ready to tell them to whom.

After the dishes were cleared and Mama went to start dinner, we all drifted to the veranda, where the breeze lifted the curtains and the scent of mango blossoms carried from the yard.

Percy and Amara played jacks in the yard with Ba. Their laughter lightened the mood, even as the grown-ups sank into conversation.

Shanti, still unmarried, sat cross-legged on the floor, plucking at her sitar with idle fingers. "Yuh see how Ba watch mi every move?" she joked. "Is like him think mi cyan even breathe without husband beside me."

Kamala laughed, a little softer. "Better him watch than forget, eh? Over by mi husband family house, mi is servant first, daughter second. All my days spent cooking for people who nuh even look my way."

Riya reached over and touched her hand. "But yuh strong, Kamala. Yuh always was."

I leaned back in the chair, arms behind my head. "An wah bout me? Everyone watching mi too, like mi a goat pon auction. Ma say is time fi wife. Ba say is time fi settle. But my head nuh deh pon that."

Shanti and Anil exchanged glances. They probably knew I was lying.

"Because yuh too busy thinking bout cricket and Papine."

The others laughed, but Riya's face grew more serious. "Still mi wish Raj was here. Family nuh feel right without him. I hope me can see him before I go back to country."

The silence that followed was heavier than cement. Even the children slowed their game, glancing up as though they felt the absence.

I cleared my throat. "We used to sit here all together, remember? Raj with his book, me teasing him til Mama shout at we. Now look, three married, two still dreaming, and me…" I trailed off.

Shanti finished for me, her voice soft. "Life change, bhai. Nutten stay the same."

We sat there for a long time, watching the sky turn pink over Franklin Town, half laughing, half grieving, bound together by love but stretched apart by the paths we had chosen.

The next morning the sun was already high by the time I reached work. Sweat clung to my back. I walked in, and to my surprise, Raj was already there. Jerome leaned against a post, grinning at us both.

“Man mi swear mi work harder when pretty woman deh pon my mind,” Jerome teased.

“Raj mi see the smile. Charmaine still cooking yuh dumpling soft?”

Raj chuckled low, shaking his head. “Mind yuh business, Jerome.”

I laughed with them. It was good to have my brother back at work. But my chest felt tight. Jerome’s words pressed on something I had been holding in. I set down my paperwork and wiped my brow.

“Mi have a gyal too, y’know.”

Raj raised an eyebrow. “Girl from Papine eh?” He smirked. “Mi know yuh eyes before yuh open yuh mouth, Pops.”

Jerome burst out laughing. “Lord, Pops finally make him mango blossom official.”

The joking died down and Raj leaned closer, his voice softer. “So yuh serious? Serious enough fi tell Ma and Ba?”

I took a deep breath. The paper in my hand felt like it weighed one thousand pounds. “Yeah, mi serious. She ah nuh just dance or secret notes. Mi want bring her home.”

Raj studied me for a long moment, then nodded. “Good. Mi hope when yuh tell them, yuh ready fi what come after. But if yuh sure, den stand firm. Love worth it.”

Jerome slapped my back. “Eh-eh, man look like the Singh brothers all fallin one by one. Mi waan be there when yuh mother hear this.”

We laughed again, but beneath it, the truth settled in my chest heavy as iron. The time had come.

Later that evening, I felt good. I don’t know if it was hope or happiness from seeing my brother at work, but I felt a sense of joy.

As I made it home, I noticed that Mama’s mood was sharper than the chilli she sprinkled into her pot. She called me into the front room, the oil lamp glowing low, her skirt pleats crisp, her face set firm.

“Pops, sit. Mi have something fi talk wid yuh,” she said.

I sat, wary.

"Yuh cousin tell mi bout a nice gyal. Hindu. Good family. Respectable. She can cook, she can sew, she carry herself proper. Mi waan yuh meet her next Sunday."

I rubbed my forehead. "Mama, mi nuh interested."

Her eyes narrowed. "Nuh interested? Yuh tink yuh is boy still? Look how yuh sister them gone. Raj gone off with him own stranger. Now yuh here wasting time with cricket and work. Yuh cyan bring shame pon mi head. Yuh haffi settle down."

"Mama," I said, voice tightening, "mi cyan marry who mi nuh love. Mi cyan tie myself to some stranger just because she fit yuh standard."

She set her hands on her hips. "Yuh sound like Raj. Yuh wan mash up all a mi prayers, all mi sacrifice, just so? Yuh think mi come to Jamaica, suffer on sugar plantation, watch mi husband fight fi turn this two room house into seven rooms, just so yuh could dash weh yuh roots? Yuh being ungrateful, Pops."

For a long moment, only the hiss of the pot in the kitchen filled the silence. Mama's lips pressed thin, her eyes glistening with unshed tears.

“One day, yuh going see mi was right,” she said, before turning away.

I sat there, chest heavy, knowing I had just crossed a line I couldn’t uncross.

Later that night, after Mama had gone to bed, I sat out on the veranda, staring at the moon hanging pale above Franklin Town. My chest still burned with her words, ungrateful, like a stone pressed down inside me.

The floorboards creaked, and Papa came out, pipe in hand. He didn’t say anything at first, just lowered himself into the chair beside me, the glow of the tobacco sparking as he drew a breath.

After a while, he said, “Yuh mother, she carry plenty weight in she heart. She dream whole life of seein yuh all married right, keepin di customs alive. But…” He paused, tapping the pipe against the armrest. “…she forget sometime dat heart can’t be ordered like grain at di market.”

I turned to him, surprised. Papa almost never spoke of such things.

He continued, his voice low but steady. “When mi was young, mi tink mi go back India. Mi promise mi own parents. But mi stay here. Jamaica hold mi. Love hold mi. An mi learn dis, life nah move by plan alone. Sometime, it choose fi yuh."

I swallowed hard. "So yuh tink mi wrong?"

Papa shook his head. "Mi tink yuh brave. But bravery come wid cost. If yuh stand, stand firm. If yuh love, love true. Dat way, when storm come, yuh cyaan be shaken."

He rose then, giving my shoulder a firm squeeze before stepping back inside, leaving me with the night sounds and his words echoing like scripture. For the first time since Mama's anger, I felt the ground under me steady.

The road to Papine felt longer that day, though my feet knew every turn by heart. The market was alive, vendors calling out about dasheen and callaloo, children chasing each other between the stalls, the air thick with spice and roasted corn. I passed it all without stopping, my thoughts heavy on what Papa had told me, on Mama's face still tight with disappointment.

When I reached the little restaurant, Devi was there as always, her hands busy over the pots, her eyes lighting when she saw me. She slipped off her apron and came outside, brushing a strand of hair from her forehead.

"Yuh look troubled, Pops," she said softly.

I laughed, a short, nervous sound. "Troubled? Maybe. But mi sure about one thing, mi cyaan keep yuh separate from mi life no more."

Her brow arched, playful. "An what yuh mean by dat?"

I took a breath, the words heavy but certain. "Mi sisters deh home now, for Papa birthday. Riya come from far, Kamala still in town before she go back to she husband yard. It feel like the right time. Devi, mi waan yuh come meet dem. Come meet Mama. Come sit at di table, see where mi from."

Her lips parted in surprise, her eyes searching mine. "Pops... yuh sure? Yuh know how people look pon families like mine, how yuh mother might look pon mi."

"Mi sure," I said, firmer now. "If mi could bring yuh into mi heart, mi can bring yuh into mi home. Dem fi see who yuh is, not jus where yuh come from."

Devi was quiet a moment, then she smiled, small but steady. "Alright. If yuh ready fi dat storm, mi walk in it wid yuh."

The market noises from outside swelled around us, but in that moment it felt like the whole world had gone still.

The Visit.

The veranda was buzzing that afternoon. Kamala was folding silks into Mama's chest, Riya was helping Shanti with her embroidery, Anil was helping Percy with his arithmetic, and Amara was playing jacks with her grandpa. The air was alive with family, voices rising and falling like a chorus.

Then I stepped through the gate with Devi.

The chatter softened, almost stopped. All eyes turned to us. Devi wore a simple cotton dress, her dupatta draped neatly, her hands folded shy at her waist. Her poise was quiet, but her eyes shone with a steadiness that eased my chest.

"Evening Ma, evening Ba," I said, clearing my throat. "Dis is my friend, Devi, from Papine."

Mama's gaze was sharp, measuring, her lips pressed tight. "Friend, eh?" she said, her tone cool.

Ba nodded, his eyes studying Devi with the same stillness he gave to weather before a storm.

Riya stood up first, her smile warm. "Welcome, sister. Come sit, nuh," she said, pulling a chair closer. Kamala followed, less sure but polite, offering Devi a sweet from the tray.

Shanti grinned from the corner, eyes wide with mischief. “So dis is di famous girl my brother always sneaking out to see?” she teased, earning a sharp look from Riya and Ma.

The children rushed forward, fearless as ever. My nephew tugged Devi’s hand. “Uncle Pops play cricket the best,” he blurted. My niece leaned on her lap, tracing the bangles on her wrist.

Devi laughed softly, settling with them, her ease like a balm in the room.

Ba cleared his throat. “Yuh family, Devi, from where?”

“Papine, sir,” she answered respectfully. “Mama is Muslim, Papa Hindu. We been in Jamaica a long time. We work hard and live quiet.”

The words hung there, firm but humble.

Mama’s eyes flicked to me, her frown deepened, but Ba only gave a slow nod, tapping his pipe against the arm of the chair.

The room began to breathe again. Kamala asked about Devi’s cooking, Riya about her brothers and sisters, the children still clinging to her. For a moment, it almost felt ordinary.

Almost.

But from the corner of my eye, I could see Ma still watching, her thoughts unreadable, her heart not yet softened.

That night, after I escorted Devi home, I returned to a quiet house. Everyone had drifted to sleep. I found Mama in the kitchen. The smell of roasted cumin lingered in the air, pots stacked neatly, the little coal stove still warm. She was wiping down the counter, her movements sharp, her sari tucked high as if even the cloth felt the weight of her mood.

"Pops," she said without looking up, "come sit."

I pulled out the stool, the same one I sat on as a boy when she taught me to roll roti. Tonight, it felt like I was back in school, waiting for a scolding.

Mrs. Singh finally turned, her eyes firm, the lamplight catching the lines time had carved into her face. "Mi want better fi yuh. Yuh a man now. Yuh haffi marry proper. Don't be like your brother. Get a Hindu girl, from good people. Good family, stable fi raise yuh up, not drag yuh down. Yuh father and me fight too hard in this foreign land fi this."

I swallowed. "Mama, Devi nuh chance. She strong, she kind, she raise up she family same way yuh did. Money nuh make heart beat."

Her hand slammed against the counter, the bangles clinking. "Love nuh cook rice, boy! Tradition keep we together. Respectable marriage protect yuh name, yuh children, yuh future. Yuh think Jamaica soft? Yuh think people nuh laugh behind we back when them see we? Yuh brother already shame me with him secret wedding. Yuh want to do the same?"

I met her eyes, chest tight but steady. I studied her for a moment. This could not be the same lady I heard stories about from my father when I was younger. The same lady who married my father when all he had were his two hands. What happened to the lady that starred in the stories I grew up hearing, the stories that made me believe in love?

"Mama, mi cyan live fi quiet yuh shame. Mi haffi live fi my own truth. If my heart say Devi, then a Devi."

The kitchen filled with silence, heavy and sharp.

Behind us, Ba's voice came, low and even. He had been standing in the doorway, pipe in hand. "Let him be, woman. Every child must choose. We can guide, but we cyan chain."

Mama spun to him, her eyes flashing. "So yuh just go sit quiet while dem throw away we name? We work hard fi mek our children remember our roots. Them just a dash weh we name."

Ba took a slow drag of the pipe, then exhaled. "Name nuh mean nothing if the house empty. Better them live happy than chained."

Mama's face tightened, but she said nothing more. She turned back to her cloth, wiping the counter again as though she could scrub the future clean.

I sat still, my chest pounding, torn between guilt and relief.

Shortly after Mama's storm, I found Ba alone in the backyard, sitting under the mango tree. The pipe glowed along with the peenie wally, while the moonlight silvered his hair. For a long while, I didn't speak, just listened to the crickets sing and the coal-quiet hum of the neighborhood settling into sleep.

Finally, he said without looking at me, "When yuh was a boy, Pops, mi used to tell yuh stories about India, nuh true?"

I nodded. "Yes Daddy. Bout the Ganges, the temple bells, the mango orchards in yuh village."

He sighed, the sound like wind through dry cane. "Mi did believe we goin back. Mi and yuh mother save every penny, dream every night. But years pass, we never mek the ship. Contract done. Jamaica hold we. An mi seh—alright, maybe mi can build India here."

I watched his hands, rough and steady. "But Mama?"

His eyes clouded. "She did love mi once—real love, like fire in dry grass. But she come here, and life harden her. Every insult from the white man, every burden of feeding ungrateful belly, every prayer unanswered, it change her. Love turn duty. Dream turn stone. She grip tradition like a rope wa keep her from drowning."

I felt my throat tighten. "So that's why she so strict bout us? Bout who we marry?"

He nodded slowly. "She think if she hold fast to old ways, we nah disappear. But she forget, yuh roots can spread in new soil too. Yuh nuh haffi chain dem to the past. Yuh mother, she live in fear. Mi… mi choose silence now."

I leaned forward. "Ba, yuh nuh silent tonight."

His mouth curved in a sad smile. "Mi ah get old. Mi tired of it. Maybe mi want yuh fi know—yuh parents was love first, duty after. Yuh mother forget that."

The night seemed to breathe with us then, the old mango leaves stirring as if carrying secrets from a homeland I had never seen but somehow always felt in my bones.

My father's words hung in the air long after he finished, as heavy as the night sky over Kingston. I sat there, feeling the weight of it—India, love, silence, fear—all braided into the man before me. For the first time, I saw not just my father, but the young man he once was, the dreamer who carried stories across the sea.

I swallowed hard. "Ba, mi nuh wan live in silence."

He looked at me, his eyes steady. "Den don't."

It was simple, but it shook me. For years, Ba had been the one who said little, the one who carried his burdens quietly. To hear him give me permission—even if he never gave himself—felt like the loosening of chains I didn't know I had been dragging.

I rose to my feet, the night air thick and warm around me. "Ba, mi love her. An mi nah go let Mama fear turn mi heart cold. If mi marry, it cyan be duty. It must be like yuh—love first, duty after."

My father pulled his pipe, a small smile creeping at the corner of his lips. "Den you go hold on to that."

The crickets carried the silence after, a kind of music between us. I walked back inside with my chest lighter, my steps firmer, and my father's blessings. For the first time, I felt like I knew what kind of man I wanted to be.

And in that quiet, I knew—after Kamala's wedding, after Raj's departure—when the dust settled, I would not just keep sneaking to Papine. I would bring Devi into my life openly, no matter the cost.

I am going to marry that girl from Papine, if she will have me of course.

CHAPTER 10 WICKETS AND WAGDAAN

I had been rehearsing all day, but by the time I sat in her living room in Papine, my tongue felt heavier than the cricket bat I once used to embarrass her brother.

Her house was buzzing. Younger siblings ran in and out with sticky mango fingers, one of her sisters was frying plantain, and her mother kept shouting at everyone to hush so she could hear me speak. Devi sat quietly at the far end, her eyes lowered but a tiny smile tugging at her lips, enjoying every bead of sweat on my forehead.

"Uncle," I started, my voice cracking, "I come fi… reason wid yuh."

Her father arched a brow. "Reason, eh? Sound like yuh in trouble already."

The younger brothers burst out laughing. "Devi, yuh bring home dis man who cyan even talk?"

I swallowed, then leaned forward. “Is nuh trouble, sah. Is love. Mi… mi love yuh daughter. Mi waan tek care of her proper, an mi askin fi yuh blessing to marry her.”

Her mother gasped loud enough to scare the chickens outside. “Marry? So fast? Is not a bag a sugar yah buy a town.”

The whole room cackled. One of the sisters clapped her hands, chanting, “Wedding! Wedding! Wedding!” while the little ones started dancing in a circle.

I tried to hold my ground, my big ears burning. “Mi serious. Is not a joke thing. Devi is my peace, an mi waan make her mi wife.”

Devi’s father leaned back, silent for a long moment. Then he rubbed his beard and said dryly, “Well, yuh brave. Brave enough fi step into a house wid ten chile an still open yuh mouth. Dat alone deserve respect.”

Her mother chimed in, “An if yuh plan fi marry her, yuh better know she wake up early every morning fi cook only yuh food. Yuh gwan eat wah the whole yard a eat.”

That broke the tension. Everyone roared with laughter. Even Devi finally looked up at me, her smile wide and mischievous, like she enjoyed watching me squirm.

Her father gave a slow nod at last. “Yuh have me blessing. But remember, love is work. More work than any field or shop. If yuh ready fi that, then me nah stop yuh. Just treat her well, love stronger than tradition.”

I exhaled so hard, everyone laughed again.

Devi just tilted her head, eyes twinkling, as if to say, *Yuh lick a six.* Relief flooded me like a cool Kingston breeze after a long day in the sun.

The next day, I asked Raj to meet me at the jewelry shop on King Street.

Raj slapped my shoulder with a grin. “Mi think yuh just mad enough fi do it. But mi proud. Devi sweet. She different.”

We leaned over glass cases, the light catching on gold bands and glittering stones. I pointed at one, a modest ring with a single diamond that glimmered without shouting.

“Dis one. It nuh need fi be plenty. Just real.”

Raj smirked. “Same like yuh heart, eh? Bold, stubborn, but true.”

We laughed, that easy laughter that softened the ache of Raj’s absence from home. For a moment, it felt like old times, brothers together, making choices that shaped their futures, daring to carve their own paths in a world that wanted to bind them.

When I stepped back into the house that evening, sweat sticking to my shirt from the Kingston sun, I swear mi whole chest was on fire, half from the heat, half from the joy bursting inside mi. I couldn't keep it in any longer. The veranda was full: Mama shelling peas, Papa sipping tea in his silence, Shanti humming like nothing in the world could trouble her.

I didn't wait. "Mama, Papa, mi go ask Devi family fi blessing… an mi get it. Mi ah go ask her to marry mi."

The words left mi mouth strong and clear, but as soon as they fell, the whole house froze. Mama's hands went stiff, peas tumbling in her lap. She stared at mi like mi was a stranger. "Marry? Yuh serious? Yuh barely know dis gyal! An what about de family we choose fi you?"

Mi heart pound, but mi didn't flinch. "Mi serious, Mama. She is de one. Her family welcome mi. Dey give mi dem word. Is time now."

Shanti chuckled soft, trying to hide it, but I caught her grin. "Bout time yuh settle down. Devi sweet, mi like her." She winked at me, like she knew exactly what Mama didn't want to hear.

Ba set down his cup, throat clearing like thunder before rain. He looked mi straight in the eye. "If yuh get de blessing from her people, den yuh must carry dis house honor when yuh join wid hers. Love is not only joy, is duty."

I nodded, feeling his words settle heavy but true. Ba didn't say much these days, but when he did, it rooted itself deep inside me.

Mama was still shaking her head, muttering, "Mash up tradition, mash up everyting…" but her voice was softer than before. I could see her eyes—the same eyes that always see mi as her favorite—full of worry, but with a little hurt pride too.

My little brother stretched out in the corner, lazy grin across his face. "Mi cyaan wait fi di wedding food."

I laughed despite the tension. For the first time in mi life, I felt like I wasn't living for them anymore, nor for tradition. This was mi story, mi choice. And I was ready.

That night, I lay on mi bed, the ceiling boards above me creaking soft with the night breeze. The house was quieter than I ever remember it. Even the crickets outside seemed hesitant to sing.

Mama's voice echoed in my mind, sharp like a cutlass, saying I mash up tradition, saying I was slipping away from everything she held on to. Every word of hers pressed heavy on my chest, because no matter how big I get, part of me always want to please her. I closed my eyes and I could still see the way her hands froze over the peas, her eyes fixed on me as if I was turning into a stranger before her very eyes.

And then there was my father's voice, calm but weighty. "Love is not only joy, is duty." Those words kept rolling round in my head like the tide at Palisadoes—coming in, pulling out, leaving me restless.

For a moment, doubt tried to slip in. What if Mama right? What if I bring shame? What if Devi and I burn bright for a while, then fade like the candle stub on my nightstand?

But then, just as fast, Devi face came to me—her shy smile at the restaurant, the sparkle in her eye when she teased me about how clumsy I was at washing dishes, the way she laughed with her whole body, head tilted back, fearless.

That memory alone pulled me back, steadied me. With her, I never felt like I was straying. I felt like I was finally finding home.

I turned on my side, pressed my forehead into the pillow, and whispered low so only the night could hear: “Tomorrow, mi start writing mi own story. Mama will learn to see mi heart. And Ba—Ba already know.”

For the first time that night, I let myself drift, half hopeful, half terrified, but certain that when morning came, I’d be one step closer to asking Devi the question that would change both our lives.

The rooster crowed before the sun even broke the sky, and still my eyes opened wide, sharper than any other morning. Usually, I’d roll over, grumble bout the noise, and wait till Mama knock on the door to remind me I had work. But not today. Today the air felt different, thick with purpose.

The house was already alive with the usual sounds: Shanti humming as she swept the veranda, pots clinking in the kitchen where Mama boiled bush tea, Ba’s cough echoing soft from his chair. It was the same house, same routine, but somehow nothing looked the same to me.

As I stepped out, my father gave me a steady nod, the kind that said more than words. Mama, on the other hand, watched me close, her eyes following me like she knew something was stirring in me she couldn't stop.

I sipped the tea, bitter and hot, and for the first time I didn't rush out the door just to escape their voices. I sat quiet, watching the morning light stretch across the yard, and I thought of Devi. Every drop of tea, every breath of the cool dawn breeze carried her name.

I knew it then, as sure as the sun coming up over the Blue Mountains. This was the beginning. Soon enough, I'd walk into that restaurant in Papine not just as a boy chasing a girl, but as a man ready to tell her, and my family, the truth of my heart.

Sunday came like a blessing. Devi lock up the restaurant early, saying she had "errands," but really it was just to meet me. We walked through Kingston slow, the kind of walk where your hands brush but don't quite hold, and every small talk turn into laughter. By the time we reached the field, the sun was hanging low, throwing long shadows across the pitch where so many matches had been fought.

I carried the cricket ball in my pocket, rolling it between my fingers like old times. "This is where I first see you proper," I told her, pointing to the crease. "Back when you mash up Barry's pride." She laughed, sweet and loud, and the sound echoed across the empty field.

We sat in the grass, the smell of cut wicket still fresh in the air. She told me stories about her siblings—who courting, who stubborn, who Mama worried over most. I told her about mine, Riya raising me and then leaving me, about Kamala moving on, Raj stirring the pot with Charmaine, and how the house felt smaller every day. She listened careful, her eyes soft, like she was carrying part of my burden for me.

When the talk grew quiet, I stood, heart thumping faster than any run I ever chased. I pulled the small box from my pocket, my hands trembling, and I swear the whole world hushed.

"Devi," I said, my voice near cracking. "Mi know life nuh simple. Mi know our families different, religion mix up, color mix up, everything. But mi heart? It settle only pon you. You more than peace to me, you the future mi want."

Her eyes widened, shining in the fading light. I dropped to one knee right there on the pitch, dust clinging to my trousers, and opened the box. The ring caught the last drop of sun like fire.

"Will you marry me?"

For a moment, she covered her mouth, like laughter and tears were fighting to come out the same time. Then she knelt too, right there in the dirt, and whispered, "Yes." Not loud, not bold, just steady, like a promise that didn't need the whole world to hear, only me.

We stayed there long after, two shadows leaning into one another, the field that once echoed with wickets and cheers now holding the start of a life together.

I still felt the weight of the ring box in my pocket when I brought Devi through our gate. I already knew how my old lady would react, but as a man, I knew what I had to do. The Sunday evening air was thick, the veranda crowded—Mama on her chair, Ba silent by the post, Shanti and Anil murmuring with curious eyes.

I cleared my throat.
"Mama, Papa… I asked Devi to marry me."

The words hung heavy. Mama's face tightened, her bangles clinking as she folded her arms.

"Marry?" Her voice cut, sharper than I expected. I wanted to fire back, but Devi just stood with quiet dignity, her chin lifted.

My father's gaze moved from me to Devi, then back. He didn't speak right away, only sighed. "The boy is grown. If he has chosen, then that is that."

Mama turned her glare on him, but he didn't budge. The silence between them was worse than shouting.

Shanti and Anil looked from one to the other, unsettled. Even Shanti, always quick with a joke, had nothing to say.

I felt my chest tighten, but I stood firm. "This is my choice, Mama. I love her. I won't change my mind."

The air in the room thickened with disappointment and unspoken words. Home suddenly felt smaller.

Her Family

Later, when we stepped into Devi's yard, everything felt different, lighter. Her family already knew me, already welcomed me as one of their own. They didn't need explanations or excuses.

Her father clapped me on the back the moment I walked in. "So, it's done then? Good! I was wondering when you would stop dragging your feet."

Her mother smiled knowingly, shaking her head. "From long time we see how you look at each other. We already gave our blessing, child. Now it's just time to plan the future."

Her sisters teased Devi until her cheeks flushed, and her younger brother grinned at me as if he were proud to be part of it.

I felt myself exhale fully for the first time all day. In their home, there was no judgment, no hesitation. Just warmth. Just love.

That night, lying awake, I thought of the two houses I had stepped into. The one that should have felt like home but was full of silence and disapproval, and the one that wasn't mine at all, yet welcomed me like blood.

One family bound by rules and old fears, the other free with love and laughter. And standing between them, I knew exactly where I wanted to build my future.

Gossip in the Village

Word spread fast through Papine and Kingston.

The middle child of Asha and Raj Sr was getting married. The shopkeeper told my mother she heard the boy marrying one gal from one mix up family. Neighbors, relatives, far and wide were expecting to be invited to this wedding.

The gossip reached York Street, making my mother more stubborn. I heard it all, but I brushed it off.

“Dem will talk today and dance tomorrow.”

In the middle of all the drama and planning, I snuck Devi away. We took a walk through Halfway Tree one evening to look at clothes and shoes. We shared bag juice and roast corn, talking about our big day.

“Yuh sure yuh family ready for me” Devi asked me.

“Ready or not, they soon find out me cyan live without yuh.”

I thought about how at night, Mama still mutters under her breath about losing control of another son, her favorite son.

“First Raj. Now Pops. Dem children nuh know weh them come from.”

“Maybe dem see where them going” Ba would usually counter her.

The house feels tense, even as wedding songs and laughter floated through the yard. Walking through the busy Halfway Tree was calm compared to York Street right now.

Later in Papine

The talk in Papine set the stage, but now the real work began.

For the first time ever, Devi was at the center of attention, and though she smiled through it, her heart was racing. She had grown up in a big household, used to cooking for siblings, nieces, and nephews, and slipping into the background so others could shine. Now the spotlight was firmly on her, and everyone had an opinion.

Her mother fussed over her dress, insisting it should be simple, respectable, nothing too bold. “Remember, Beti, you walking in church, before God.”

Her sisters and cousins, on the other hand, teased and argued over fabrics. “She must wear lace. English wedding have lace.”

Her brothers, not to be left out, chimed in about the food. “Devi, make sure the goat can do. And keep the sorrel cold.”

Through it all, she felt her cheeks warm whenever she thought of him, the middle son, bold and smiling, slipping away from Franklin Town just to sit in her family’s yard and talk with her father. When he asked for her hand, she had never felt so seen, so chosen.

But with being chosen came the weight of expectation. Devi’s family was easy, open, mixing Muslim and Hindu traditions with island ways. But she had heard whispers about his mother, how stern she was, how much she clung to custom. And now, as wedding plans crossed between church pews and tassa drums, Devi knew her steps would either bridge two families or break them further apart.

At night, she lay in bed listening to the crickets outside, her hand tracing the simple ring he had given her. She prayed, half in Hindi, half in English, for strength. She prayed she would be more than just the girl from Papine. She prayed she would be enough.

CHAPTER 11 GOSPEL. DHOLAK. AND SKA

The hard part was over. Standing up firm to my old lady was the hard part, or so I thought.

Time to plan the wedding.

It was decided that the best place for both families to meet was Papine, neutral, bustling, and familiar. I also thought it was good for my mother to see how different people can live in one house.

The restaurant Devi's brother owned closed its doors for a special lunch, the long tables set with enamel plates and bright sorrel in jars, a mix of simplicity and celebration.

On one side of the table sat my family. Ma stiff as a board, arms folded across her chest. Ba quiet as usual. All my sisters, even the married ones, whispering among themselves. Jerome trying to lighten the mood with little jokes.

On the other side, Devi's family leaned into the gathering with laughter, chatter, and easy smiles. Her father booming with warmth, her mother with sharp but kind eyes, her siblings teasing each other loudly as if the whole thing was a Sunday picnic.

My mother started the conversation. "Wedding must be proper. Hindu ways. Priests, mantras, the whole thing." She spoke like it was a decree, her jaw set tight.

She was insistent on a Hindu wedding, complete with pundit, sacred fire, mantra, and a proper mandap.

Devi's mother leaned forward, calm but firm. "Our daughter will not be left out of her own marriage. There will be food from both sides, prayers from all three faiths. And love first, because that is what brought them together."

Devi's father chuckled, trying to ease the sting. "Look here now, Asha, you going get your grandchildren either way. You can't quarrel with love."

"Love alone don't keep a house, Mr. Jones."

I could feel the weight pressing down. My palms sweated under the table, but when Barry winked at me, it eased some of the nerves.

Ba finally cleared his throat. "We can't cuss in front of the children. Let the boy have his wedding. Let both families bring their prayers. God will hear them all."

That broke some of the tension. Her sisters laughed and whispered about saris and gowns. Jerome leaned over to Devi's brothers and started a loud conversation about cricket and music. Even Ma, though still stiff, leaned back in her chair and didn't argue again.

For me, sitting between both families, it was like standing in two different Jamaicas. One was holding on to the old ways. The other opening its door wide to change. And right there in Papine, with the clatter of cutlery and the smell of curry and roti between us, I realized the wedding would be more than vows.

It was a bridge. Between Hindu, Christianity, and Islam. Between Indian and Black. Between tradition and something new.

The next day, my family and I sat with each other at breakfast.

Ba broke the silence. "We cyan fight the whole way to the wedding," he said, sipping his tea. "Better unu find middle ground before the whole ting mash up."

So the families met again, this time with lists.

Devi's sisters wanted music and dancing, lots of it. Mama wanted rituals to bless the union. Devi herself said gently, "I don't want a war at my wedding. I want peace. I want something that feels like both of us."

The idea was floated: two ceremonies, side by side. But the logistics quickly spiraled. Who would come, which priest, which imam, which costs. Voices rose again.

The turning point came in a private conversation. I sat with Devi the following week beneath a mango tree outside the restaurant.

"Love, if we let them decide everything, we'll never marry at all," I whispered.

She smiled faintly. "So what do we do?"

I took her hand. "We make it our way. One wedding. One vow. Everyone else will just have to bend."

And so the idea was born. A Christian wedding in a church, in English, clear, neutral, understandable for all, with vows we both could say.

Followed by a grand Indian reception, full of food, music, and tradition, but infused with island flavor. Curries, roti, jerk chicken, punch, tabla, dholak, alongside mento and ska.

She smiled at me and offered the sweetest chups on my cheek.

I felt like I took the weight off her shoulders with that suggestion.

Breaking the News

When the decision was announced, the room nearly split.

Mama was furious. "Christian? In a church? That's not our way."

Devi's mother countered, "And not ours either. But at least it not erasing one side."

Ba, as always, was steady. "If the boy and girl happy, then let it be so. None of we living their marriage for them."

Even Barry cracked a joke—"At least now I can wear one good English suit instead of all them hot kurta ting."

Slowly, with sighs and mutters, both families accepted.

It was decided.

The wedding would be held in a small Anglican church in Kingston—stone walls, wooden pews, sunlight through stained glass windows. We will have bridesmaids and groomsmen. Devi will wear white. The vows would be simple.

Afterwards, the real celebration would begin. A reception that was neither one culture nor the other but both: saris and lehengas swirling alongside Sunday best, dhol, drums and tassam ixed with calpyson, mento, and ska, garlands of marigold and bougainvillea hung side by side.

The older generation fretted, but the younger ones cheerted. For them, it wasn't betrayal—it was Jamaica itself, alive and blended, making something new.

Later that week I sat with Raj, Anil, Jerome, Percy and a few more cousins on Jerome's veranda.

Jerome poured the whites into my cup like ah water.

"So who brave enough fi stand beside yuh when Devi family start eyeing down we side?"

Jerome cracked.

Anil jumped up, puffing up with pride. "Me can do it."

Raj laughed, "yuh cyan even keep track of yuh shoes, much less the ring."

After much back and forth, I decided in my mind who my best man would be.

I leaned back, grinning at everyone. My eyes settled on Raj, quiet in the corner with a cigarette half lit. our eyes met. And in that silent exchange, I felt all the years we shared—from sharing a bed, to playing cricket in the yard, to sneaking out, to late night whispers about love and family.

It has to be him.

"My best man will be Raj."

The laughter died down, replaced with nods, and knowing glances. Raj stubbed out his cigarette and smirked, trying to play it cool, but everyone can see the pride in his eyes.

"Bout time yuh trust yuh big brother," Jerome muttered. "Now we really have a wedding."

It was decided. Raj, Jerome, Anil, and Percy, my messenger, will stand with me on that fated day.

Later that night, during our walk back to Franklin Town, before Raj would take the left to Allman Town, we shared a quiet moment.

The crickets hummed, and the smell of damp earth rose after a short rain shower.

"So," Raj finally said, breaking the silence, "you really tust me to stand up next to you? After all the times me get yuh in a trouble?"

"Trouble I was happy for big brother. Trouble I asked for. And yuh the only one I could trust not to drop the ring or mash up the speech."

Raj's smirk softened into something almost solemn. He tapped ash into the night.

"Marriage ah nuh just dance and pretty clothes, yuh know? Is two people deciding to fight through all the rough days together. Ma and Ba teach we dat in two different ways. Ba with silence, Ma with stubbornness. But them still there. Side by side. Don't forget that when yuh vex."

I leaned back, studying him. "yuh sound like a man wa know love proper."

Raj didn't answer right away. He just smiled, a half-secret smile that made the night heavier.

"Charmaine and I are having a baby. I learned a thing or two by now."

I stopped in my tracks. My face turned into a wide grin.

He was smiling like a old crook now.

"Congrats, someone else to call me "uncle pops" now."

He looked at me again, eyes softened. "Mi happy. More than mi ever imagine."

"Just remember this Pops, don't marry just for custom or to please anybody else. You choose love, you live love. If you sure bout Devi, hold on tight, cause life ah go test yuh."

For the first time in a long time, Raj looked like the older brother I remembered—steady, serious, and protective. And in that moment, I felt certain I chosen the right man to stand beside me.

I clapped his shoulder, eyes bright. "Dis a the best news Raj. Forget all Ma's vexation, forget tradition. Life find a way eh? You make your own family now."

For once my brother let his joy show fully. Walking back together in the half light- I felt our bond deepen—one brother preparing for marriage, the other for fatherhood. Both of us, in our own ways, defying the path our mother wanted, and finding our own happiness.

Gossip in the village

Word spread fast through Papine and Kingston.

The middle child of Asha and Raj Sr, is getting married. The shop keeper told My mother she heard the boy marrying one gal from one mix up family.

Neighbors, relatives, far and wide were expecting to be invited to this wedding.

The gossip reached York Street, making my mother more stubborn. I heard it all, but I brush it off.

"Dem will talk today and dance tomorrow."

In the middle of all the drama and planning, I snuk Devi away. We took a walk through halfway tree one evening to look at clothes and shoes.

We shared bag juice and roast corn, talking about our big day.

"Yuh sure yuh family ready for me?" Devi asked me.

"Ready or not, they soon find out me cyan live without yuh."

I thought about how At night, Ma still mutters under her breath about losing control of another son; her favorite son.

"First Raj. Now Pops. Dem children nuh know weh them come from."

"Maybe dem see where them going," Ba would usually counter her.

The house feels tense, even as wedding songs and laughter floated through the yard. Walking through the busy half way tree, was calm compared to York street right now.

Later in Papine

The talk in Papine set the stage, but now the real work began.

For the first time ever, Devi was at the center of attention—and though she smiled through it, her heart was racing. She had grown up in a big household, used to cooking for siblings, nieces, and nephews, and slipping into the background so others could singe. Now the spotlight was firmly on her, and everyone had an opinion.

Her mother fussed over her dress—insisting it should be simple, respectable, nothing too bold. " Remember, Beti, you walking in church, before God."

Her sisters and cousins, on the other hand, teased and argued over fabrics. "She must wear lace! English wedding have lace."

Her brothers, not to be left out, chimed in about the food.

"Devi, make sure the goat can do. And keep the sorrel cold."

Through it all, she felt her cheeks warm, whenever she thought of him—the middle son, bold and smiling, slipping away from Franklin Town just to sit in her family's yard and talk with her father. When he asked for her hand, she had never felt so seen, so chosen.

But with being chosen came the weight of expectation. Devi's family was easy, open mixing muslim and Hindu traditions with island ways. But she had heard whispers about his mother—how stern she was, how much she clung to custom. And now, as wedding plans crossed between church pews and tassa drums, Devi knew her steps would either bridge two families or break them further apart.

At night, she lay in bed listening to the crickets outside, her hand tracing the simple ring he had given her. She prayed—half in hindi, half in English for streght. She prayed she would be more than just the "girl from papine." She prayed she would be enough.

CHAPTER 12 FROM CHURCH BELLS TO TASSA DRUMS

My house was alive long before the sun rose, every corner buzzing with preparations. Aunties shuffled in and out with trays of sweets. Cousins carried out chairs and flowers, and the smell of curry, ghee, and fried fish drifted through the windows. The yard was strung with bamboo poles for garlands and children ran between them as if it were already a festival.

Inside, my sisters sat at the mirror, oiling hair, and pressing saris and gowns for tomorrow. The chatter around was cheerful, yet there was a lingering silence everyone felt but no one spoke of. The day felt heavy. Tomorrow was not just any wedding, it was mine. I tried to keep my head low, helping, but I could feel the stares. The little ones trailed after me, whispering questions about my bride. My sisters teased me, saying Devi would need all the patience in the world. And my mother, my mother watched me with sharp eyes, never saying much, but always calculating.

By midday, Raj, Jerome, and a few cousins found me on the back veranda.

“Nervous?” Jerome asked, grinning like the devil. I brushed him off, but inside my chest felt tight. Raj, always serious, clapped my shoulder and reminded me, “You alright. You chose love. Not everyone gets to.” His words steadied me, especially coming from him, who had done the same with Charmaine.

As evening came, the air shifted. The cousins sang Bhojpuri folk songs while stringing marigold, the smell of curry and fried plantain drifting in the air. I sat with Ba on the step as he smoked his pipe. He didn't say much, only asked if I was sure. I told him I was, that Devi was not only my peace but my partner, and I'd rather have her by my side in hardship than anyone else in comfort. He gave me a small nod, and that was enough.

Later in the quiet of my room, I took out the ring box from its hiding place. It still felt unreal that she had told me yes on the cricket field, that tomorrow the promises would be sealed before both families and the world. I smiled, thinking of her laughter, her stubbornness, her care for her family, and the way she carried herself with humility and fire.

Outside, the house pulsed with song and preparation, but inside me there was a calm.

Papine the Day Before

The morning sun poured through the windows of her family's wooden house in Papine, catching on the freshly polished brass lotas and trays laid out for the rituals.

Devi woke up early, not because she was told to, but because sleep had abandoned her. The thought that tomorrow she would no longer just be her father's daughter or Barry's sister, but someone's wife, left her with both a flutter in her chest and a tremor in her hands.

Her mother fussed over her, oiling her hair with coconut and lavender and weaving jasmine flowers into its length.

"You must shine tomorrow," she said, though Devi could sense the layers beneath her mother's words. Joy for her daughter, sadness at the parting, and the quiet pride of seeing her marry with both families' blessings.

The house was crowded with siblings and cousins. Her sisters argued over gowns and saris. Her brothers teased her and the littlest ones peeked in the door, whispering as though she had suddenly become a queen. Devi tried to laugh along, but she felt like her whole body was alive with nerves.

By midday, aunts gathered to prepare sweetmeats and apply mehendi to her hands. They drew vines, peacocks, and flowers, each curve and swirl a blessing for love and fertility. As they worked, they told her stories of their own weddings, some arranged, some love matches, each with its own lessons hidden in laughter. Devi listened closely, stealing moments to think of him, the man who had chosen her, not by arrangement, but with his heart.

In the late afternoon, her closest brother slipped into the room with a grin and whispered that Percy was here. Just knowing he was thinking of her on this day of all days steadied her. She held the note close, not daring to read it aloud, but the sight of his familiar scrawl made her lips curve into a smile.

As night fell, her father called her outside to sit on the veranda. The lamp burned low, peenie wally danced in the yard, and he spoke to her in a steady voice about marriage. “Remember, Devi, marriage is not only love, but patience, respect, and sacrifice. If you can keep laughter at home, you will be rich.” She leaned her head against his shoulder, silent tears slipping down, feeling the weight of her new life ahead.

Inside, the women sang old bhajan wedding songs, their voices rising into the humid night. Tomorrow she would step into a different world, but tonight, she was still Devi of Papine, daughter, sister, middle child, and beloved girl of her home.

The church was filled long before we arrived. Aunties in bright saris and cousins in pressed suits fanned themselves with folded programs, the murmur of gossip and excitement rippling through the pews. The whitewashed walls seemed to hum with the toll of the bells, each note pulling the guests to silence as the organ began its hymn.

I stood at the front with Raj, Jerome, Anil, and Percy. I heard the bells toll, each peal sending a tremor through my chest. I stood at the little Anglican church in Kingston, my palms damp despite the cool stone floor beneath my feet. The air smelled of lilies and candle wax, and outside I could hear the tassa drums warming up, waiting for us when this part was done.

I imagined this moment for weeks.

The doors opened and there she was, and everything fell away. The crowd, the whispers, even my mother's stiff face in the pew. All I saw was her.

My bride entered slowly, veiled, her gown simple but radiant, English lace softened by an island sunbeam slipping through stained glass. I stood waiting, my hands heavy.

Finally our eyes met across the aisle. Kingston seemed to hold its breath at that very moment. She looked nervous but certain. When our eyes found each other, I knew every risk, every fight, every sleepless night was worth it.

The pastor's voice rose solemn yet warm, asking us to repeat ancient vows. I thought of my father's silence at the kitchen step, of my mother's disapproval, of the gossip. But I also thought of Devi's family sitting proudly in the front row, her mother's soft smile, her father's chin lifted with pride. They had welcomed me despite my own family's struggles. They had given us their blessing.

My voice shook at first, but then steadied. I promised to love her, to stand by her, to protect her, even when the world pushed back. And when she repeated her words in that soft but stubborn tone of hers, I felt my knees weaken.

The ring slid onto her finger, the same ring I hid in my mattress, the same one I had turned over in my hand a hundred times. My hand lingered longer than it should have, my thumb brushing against hers. She squeezed back, just once, enough to tell me she was here, truly mine.

The pastor declared us husband and wife, and the bells erupted again. Raj clapped me on the back, the congregation cheered, and outside, the tassa drum responded, fierce and joyful. I leaned forward and kissed her, and for the first time in my life, I felt entirely free.

I looked out at my family, some happy, some still stiff, my mother unreadable, but I did not falter. Devi's hand was in mine, her heart steady, and together we turned toward the sunlight streaming through the doors, ready to step into whatever future Jamaica had waiting for us.

If the church had been soft candlelight and solemn promises, the reception was fire.

As soon as we stepped into the yard in Papine, the tassa drums exploded, the rhythm running up my spine, shaking me from the inside. The air was thick with curry, jerk, smoke, and the sweet burn of rum. Children darted between tables, women in bright saris and headwraps fanned themselves, and old uncles were already arguing over cricket.

Devi's hands were still in mine, but now she laughed free and unguarded, her white dress catching streaks of turmeric and rum as family pressed food into our hands. Someone smeared powder on my cheek, someone else shoved a drink at me. My cousins hoisted me up before I could protest, chanting my name, while Devi blushed as her sisters teased her about the wedding night.

I looked across the crowd through the dancers and saw my father sitting quietly, content in the shade with a drink, while my mother's lips stayed tight as she watched the tassa players whip the drums faster. Still, even she couldn't keep her eyes off Devi's glow, or the way the crowd embraced her.

The dancers put on a show, a mix of Indian hand movements and island sway, skirts twirling, bangles clinking, as congas joined the tassa. My people and Devi's people were clapping to the same beat. Different worlds now tangled in the same rhythm. It felt like a bridge, something larger than both of us.

Later, when I pulled Devi close for our first dance, "Since I Met You Baby" played over the speakers. The crowd cheered and stomped, and for a moment the whole yard seemed to move with us. She whispered she couldn't believe this was real, and I whispered that it was only the beginning.

I knew there were still some storms ahead, the disapproval, the gossip, the weight of our different worlds, my duty as a son and brother. But standing there, the drums at our backs, Devi's hand in mine, I felt like Jamaica itself was blessing us.

When the night wound down and the drums finally softened, I stepped outside for a breath. The church bells of the morning still echoed faintly in my memory, as if their quiet dignity had followed me here, now colliding with the heat and thunder of tassa drums. Two sounds that should not belong together, but somehow did, like Devi and me.

I thought of Raj and Charmaine, of Kamala in her husband's house, of Rosie and her family, Mama's silence, and Ba's tired smile. Families had been broken and rebuilt in the span of months, but standing there with Devi's hand in mine, I felt like we had forged something new, something that didn't erase where we came from but refused to be bound by it.

The bells rang for tradition. The drums beat for change. And between them, in that fragile middle ground, was where our love would live.

CHAPTER 13 THE SECOND MOTHER

It's been almost a year since the wedding. The seasons of Kingston have passed: one more mango crop, one more cricket season, one more round of gossip in the verandas of Franklin Town. Devi now belongs to this house, her laugh mingling with Shanti's chatter and the sound of Ba's radio humming in the evenings. But it is not without strain. Living under my mother's eyes is never easy.

Devi has proven herself capable, cooking roti that even my mother admits tastes like back home, keeping the house in order, winning the affection of my niece and nephews, including my now four-month-old nephew who visits every now and then. Yet there are still quiet moments of judgment from Ma, who reminds me, sometimes directly, sometimes in whispers, of the good Hindu girls from wealthy families I could have chosen.

For me though, the house feels warmer with Devi. Coming home from work, I find her presence the balm I always longed for, the peace after the noise of the day. We share late night talks on the veranda, where I learned more about her parents' struggles, Hindu father, Muslim mother, who taught her that love always bends tradition even if it does not break it.

The absence of Raj still hangs like a shadow. He's still in town, but sometimes it feels like he's worlds away. Kamala writes letters from her in-law's house, filling us in on her expected bundle of joy. Riya is still sending her love and heart with Amara and Percy to keep us company. Shanti watches Devi closely, perhaps admiring her courage and wondering if she too can choose her own path. Anil still dreams aloud, still restless.

I woke before the rooster crowed. The house was already alive with sound. Not the sharp commands of Mama or the cough of Ba's pipe this time, but Devi's voice, soft and steady, humming an old tune as she stirred the pot in the kitchen. The smell of plantain, callaloo, and dumpling drifted down the hallway, a scent that felt like home.

The floorboards creaked as my niece and nephew tiptoed past my door, chasing after her, giggling because they knew she would slip them a sweet before breakfast. I stretched out on my bed listening, Mama's pots clattering a little sharper than necessary, Ba clearing his throat but saying nothing, the rhythm of a house that shifted since Devi moved in.

When I stepped onto the veranda, the morning breeze cooling my face, I saw her through the open shutters, blouse tucked, hair pinned neat, her hands moving with purpose. She was not just a visitor anymore. She was a part of the walls, the yard, the heartbeat of this place. And though my mother's eyes lingered too long on her, heavy with unspoken judgment, I knew the house was warmer now, steadier. With Devi here, even silence felt full.

Sometimes Ma still acted like she had something to prove. Some mornings before the sun cleared the breadfruit tree, she called Devi into the kitchen with a sharp voice, handing her tasks one after another.

"Sweep the yard, wash down the veranda, see to the dhal."

It was as if Mama had forgotten she had another daughter or her own hands, or maybe she wanted to see if Devi would bend or break.

But Devi never once complained. She moved through the house steady and graceful, as if the work belonged to her hands alone. She cooked the roti thin, soft, and tender, fried plantains crisp and golden, and stirred curry with the same patience she used when braiding Amara's hair. She laughed with the children as she washed their clothes, and when they cried, it was her lap they now sought.

At times, I watched from the doorway, half proud and half ashamed. Proud that she carried herself so well in a house that was not always kind to her, ashamed that Mama treated her more like a helper than family.

Still, Devi found ways to make the house her own. She planted little herbs by the side of the yard, thyme, scallion, mint, and soon enough even Mama reached for them while cooking. She sang softly as she worked, her voice floating through the rooms, making the house feel like a home in ways no one could deny.

The truth was clear. Though Mama tried to test her, it was Devi who held the house together now.

I remember a few weeks ago after supper, Mama pulled me aside in the kitchen after I returned from work, her voice low but sharp. The pots still steamed, Devi humming softly as she washed them out by the pipe.

"Pops," she said, her kerchief on her head shifting as she folded her arms and snapped her head, "yuh wife too free.

She act like this is her house. This is your house now. She not like us. You spoil her and she forget her place."

Her words stung, not because they were true, but because I had heard them before, whispered by neighbors, muttered by distant cousins.

I bit back my anger. "Mama, Devi work harder than anyone in this yard. She cook, she clean, she take care of the children. What more yuh want from her?"

For the first time in my life, I saw my mother's eyes flash. "Respect and humbleness."

Before I could answer, a small voice broke in. Amara stood barefoot in the doorway, holding the hem of her dress.

"Grandma," she said softly, "Aunty Devi braid my hair today. She nice to me."

Behind her, Percy stood firmly, adding, "she tell we story too. Bout her family."

From the veranda, Ba's voice drifted in, steady as always. "The house run better since she come."

He didn't step into the room. He didn't look at us. He didn't need to. His words connected like stones.

Mama pressed her lips tight, clattered a pot louder than needed, and walked away without answering.

I stood there a moment longer, watching Devi at the pipe, her sleeves wet to the elbows, her voice still humming as if she hadn't heard a word. She had, I knew she had, but she carried herself with the grace of someone who refused to bend to bitterness.

That night, lying awake, I realized what Mama called "too free" was exactly what made me love Devi: her strength, her laughter, her kindness, and her refusal to shrink. And maybe everyone else would eventually see it too.

By the time I went back to the veranda, Ba was still in his chair, pipe as usual, though lately he barely lit it. His cough had grown deeper these past months, and he moved slower now, his eyes heavier, but still he sat at the head of the yard like a man who refused to surrender his place. He nodded at me, not speaking, but the gesture was more than enough.

Mama clattered in and out of the kitchen, barking orders. Devi answered only with a calm "yes Ma," moving with quiet efficiency, the children trailing after her like ducklings.

Percy tugged at my shirt. “Uncle Pops, yuh going work already? Play cricket nuh before yuh leave.” My niece clung to Devi’s skirt, already begging for more stories.

I smiled and kissed their heads. “Work call me, but when I come back, I’ll play a match.”

Breakfast was a mix of order and chaos, Papa’s cough breaking the silence, Mama sighing over every detail not done her way, Devi gently serving plates to each person before she sat for herself. I ate quickly, the clock already pulling me toward the shop.

As I slung my bag over my shoulder and stepped into the yard, the sound of the laughter followed me. Devi stood at the doorway, wiping her hands on her apron, her smile steady despite Mama’s watchful eyes. And Papa, tired but proud, raised his hand in a slow blessing as I headed down the road into Kingston’s bustle.

The house carried on behind me, a place both warm and strained, filled with duty, laughter, and love, all pressed into the same morning.

The factory was already buzzing by the time I arrived, the morning sun baking the street outside, the smell of tobacco and smoke that clung to our skin long after we left. Machines rattled and hissed, cutting, rolling, pressing cigarettes by the thousands. The foreman barked orders from across the room, his voice fighting the clatter of iron gears.

Raj worked with his head down, steady hands feeding paper into the rolling machine. He had always been the quiet one, careful, methodical. Beside him Jerome whistled through his teeth, flirting with the girls on the packing line, making them giggle even as they stacked cartons high.

I stood near the press, looking over invoices, sweat sticking my shirt to my back, the roar of the rollers in my ears. Work was heavy, but the rhythm of it gave us time to talk between the noise.

Jerome leaned in, shouting over the machinery. "So Raj, how Charmaine and Jo doing? Still glowing and keeping you up a night time?"

Raj didn't look up, just smirked. "They doing good. Jo start creeping and want climb now."

I laughed, the sound swallowed by the machines. "Yuh wan act cool but me see the pride pon yuh face."

"And you married a good year now. Still alive. Devi a feed yuh good?"

"Feeding me, keeping the house together, making things less sour than usual," I said, wiping sweat from my brow. "But my old lady still treat her like she a the helper. Every day a new test. Devi nuh bend though."

Raj finally looked up, his expression serious.
"Good. Don't let Mama's fire cool yuh marriage. Devi strong, but even strong hearts get tired."

After that day, it felt like donkey years before the bell rang. We wiped our hands, smoke rising from the machines as they slowed. For a moment, the three of us stood together in the haze of tobacco dust, brothers bound not just by blood but the grind of labor and friendship.

We stepped out into the Kingston evening, shirts clinging to our backs, hands still smelling of smoke and paper.

Jerome stretched, groaning. "Lawd, mi feel like mi lungs full a cigarette already." He laughed, but Raj didn't join in. His face was shadowed, quiet.

As we walked toward our side of Kingston, before he would turn to Allman Town and me to Franklin Town, he finally spoke.
"Yuh notice Ba slowing down more lately? When I dropped off Jo the other day to visit unu, I saw it."

I nodded. "Yeah. His cough worse. He barely light the pipe these days, just hold it, like the smoke too heavy now."

Raj kicked a stone along the road, frowning. "Ma act like she don't see it. She keep him busy in the yard, like if she nuh admit it, it nah happen."

"Me worry say one day we just a go find him like that. Gone."

The thought sat heavy between us. None of us wanted to say it, but it was true. Ba had carried silence all his life, but now his silence was sickness too.

I shoved my hands in my pockets, trying to push away the fear. "We cyan't lose him yet. Not while the house still feel empty with you gone, Kamala gone, Riya gone. We need him. Even if all he does now is sit and nod."

Raj glanced at me, his eyes steady. "Den we look after him. We make sure he know someone is watching, even if Mama don't say the words."

"One day I have to learn to be a father, and mi nuh ready fi that bro."

We walked on in silence after that, the smoke of the factory still clinging to our clothes, the weight of the family heavier than any sack I ever lifted.

By the time I reach Franklin Town, the light was low and the yard was still. And there he was, just where I knew he'd be, sitting on the front step, his pipe unlit in his hand, coughing into a rag he thought nobody noticed. He looked smaller somehow, like the years had finally caught up with him all at once.

"Mek yuh reach, son," he said, his voice rough but steady.

I set down my bag and sat beside him. For a moment, we didn't speak, just listened to the crickets starting their songs. Devi's voice drifted from the kitchen, calling the children to wash their hands. The smell of fried fish wrapped the house in comfort.

"Ba," I said at last, "yuh must rest more. Leave the yard work to me."

He shook his head, slow and stubborn. "If I stop moving, boy, I gone already."

He sighed. "Let me sit here, let me feel the yard alive around me."

I looked at him, at the lines etched deep into his face, and felt something twist in my chest. I wanted to argue, but instead I just nodded. Sometime the silence was the only answer a son could give his father.

Later that night, the house was hushed after dinner. The children finally drifted to sleep, the yard lay still under the stars, and only the sound of Ba's coughing broke the silence every now and then.

Devi and I sat together in our room, the small lamp throwing a circle of light against the wall. She was folding away clothes, her movements slow, her brow furrowed in thought. I watched her a long while before she finally spoke.

"Your father… he's not well." Her voice was soft, but there was no hesitation. "I see it when he stand, when he walk, even the way he hold the pipe. It's not age."

I sighed, leaning back on the bed. "I know. He weaker every day for the last few months. But Ma, she act like she don't see it. Every morning she push him to do this and that."

Devi looked at me then, her eyes steady, her hands folded in her lap. "She love him in her own way, but denial is not love. If you don't face the sickness, it take him faster."

Her words cut because they were true. I thought of Ba coughing into a rag, pretending to clear his throat when he thought no one was watching. I thought of Mama clattering pots louder than needed, as if the noise could drown out the truth.

Devi reached across and placed her hand on mine. "We must be the ones to see to him, really see him. The children already do. They run to him softer now, like they know he fragile. Maybe you need to talk to Raj Jr, Riya, and Kamala. Yuh cyan carry it alone."

I pressed her hand, grateful for her calm. "Yuh right. Tomorrow I'll talk to Raj. I'll get a courier to contact Kamala and Riya too."

Her smile was small but firm. "Good. Family need to hold on to each other when hard time come."

As Devi fell asleep in my arms, I thought about this past year. Devi was no longer "the girl from Papine" in the eyes of most of my reasonable relatives. She had become Second Mother.

When cousins from St. Mary or Spanish Town dropped in, it was Devi they called for food. When the children scraped knees or quarreled in the yard, they ran to her skirts before anyone else. Aunties whispered to her that her roti was softer than anyone's, that her hand with the dhal tasted like home. Even the neighbors leaned across the fence to ask her advice on herbs, children, on small troubles.

I thought about last week, the house swelled with visitors—cousins crowding the veranda, uncles playing cards under the breadfruit tree, nieces darting between rooms. Devi moved among them calm and smiling, ladling curry onto plates, smoothing hair, telling stories that made the little ones giggle.

"Second Mother!" one of my younger cousins squealed, tugging at her hand. "Tell us the story of the boat again!"

Devi laughed, her eyes lighting up. "Only if yuh promise to eat your food first." The yard erupted in laughter, the title catching on every tongue until it seemed everyone was calling her by it.

From the corner of the room, I caught Mama watching. Her lips pressed tight, her bangles still. She said nothing, but the shadow in her eyes was clear. She had spent years holding this house together, keeping the children fed and clothed, the name intact. And now, without even trying, Devi had taken the light from her.

I slipped my hand over Devi's while she slept. She had found her place in this family—not by demand, not by tradition, but by selfless love. And that was something no one could erase.

CHAPTER 14: WHEN THE HOUSE LEANS

By early summer, the house was swelling again with the sound of babies. Kamala visited with her daughter—lungs so strong you could hear them coming from down the road, curls already framing her tiny head. As she reached the gate with Lilly, she placed her directly in Devi's arms without asking. Devi rocked her like she was her own, sang lullabies under her breath, and moved through the house with ease. The children clearly adored her. My sisters praised her, and I nodded with respect and pride.

Raj Jr and Charmaine even dropped by with Jo more often to see Ba. That little boy is going to be feisty like his uncle Pops. Already he want run before he can walk properly. It was nice seeing them come by more often, especially since I discussed Ba with him.

Riya even came to town. She came with a surprise this time—a belly that looked like it held the whole a Cockburn Pen in it. She was due this October. It was like little by little, the family was getting accustomed to our new lives.

Then it happened.

Ba's body gave way. It came sudden, the second to last Sunday in August. One afternoon, while sitting in his chair on the veranda, his words slurred, his pipe slipping from his hand. The yard froze. The children bawled out. Mama shouted his name. By the time Anil and I carried him inside, one side of his face gone slack, his legs dragging heavy.

I had been begging him for weeks to go to Public with me. But the bull inside of him would not move.

The doctor came, spoke words like "stroke" and "rest," but all we could see was Ba's silence deepening. His walk was crooked, his voice halved to whispers. The man who always looked brave, his eyes were now wide and scared, though he said nothing we could make sense of. His hands kept curling in on themselves like they no longer obeyed him.

The house shifted overnight. Ma wept to her cousins or to herself in the room. She thought by now we would be getting ready to arrange Shanti's suitors for the Christmas season. Eventually she began to insist he try to walk, to talk, to swallow his food. I think by then her fear wore the mask of anger.

It was Devi though who became his caretaker. She fed him slowly, spoon by spoon, like she did with Jo or Lilly. She woke earlier, set the water to boil, carried a tray with bush tea and soft bread. She hummed lullabies to him, rubbed his stiffened limbs with oil, helped me steady him when it was bath time. At night she wrapped him in a blanket before the evening breeze swept through the shutters, and if the cough shook him awake, she was there before Ma stirred.

His eyes softened around her. He might not have had the words anymore, but the way his hand trembled to pat hers spoke more than language.

Even the children began to call for her before anyone else, clinging to her clothes as if she was the only steady ground left.

Everything felt different after Ba's stroke. Before, he would rise early, sweep the veranda, light his pipe, and watch the street wake up. Now, he sat slumped in his chair, words tangled into sounds that were hard to decipher.

Even though Devi looked like she had things under control, I noticed that when the house was still, her shoulders slumped, her eyes turned toward the hills. Sometimes she would pause with her hands in the basin, staring at the water as if it might show her another place.

One evening, after the children had gone to bed and the house had fallen quiet, I found her sitting on the veranda steps, her face lit by moonlight.

"You miss them, don't you?" I asked.

Her eyes filled, but her smile held. "Every day. My mother, my father, my brothers, my sisters. I dream sometimes I am back home, in the yard with them. I smell my mother's cooking, I hear my father's laugh. Then I wake up, and it's gone."

I sat beside her, pulling her close. "We can visit," I said, though we both knew it was not going to be that simple. For her, I would try. But the work, the children, my father, the distance, the weight of this house—all of it pressed down.

I felt guilty. It was never supposed to be like this. What started out as a two-room house on York Street was now a seven-bedroom house with ample space. Raj Jr, Charmaine, and Jo should be here too. If Raj was here with me, I would feel better about leaving them home for a few days to visit Devi's family. Raj left to protect Charmaine. I am now the man of the house. Anil still in school, he can barely walk straight much less watch over things.

She probably felt my guilt. She leaned against me. "This is my home now. But sometimes it feel like I have two families. One here, one there. And I can't be in both."

Her voice cracked then, just once, before she steadied herself.

I pulled her close, feeling the weight of what she never said aloud in daylight. She still rose before dawn as always, to tend to my father, to cook, to iron, to hold the house together. But here, under the stars, she was simply a daughter missing home.

A few days later, the relatives came by in a crowd—aunties with baskets of fruit, cousins loud with chatter, children running wild in the yard. And once again, it was my wife, Devi, they swarmed to.

"Second Mother, yuh roti soft like butter," my little cousin said as he took a second plate.

Even the men nodded as she poured drinks and kept the table flowing.

She smiled as usual.

That night, as the house quieted after the gathering, I lay awake with two truths pressing on me. Devi had become the pillar of this family—strong enough to steady even Ba's faltering steps. But beneath her smile was longing, the ache of a woman who still carried the hills of Papine in her chest.

And I wondered how long she could hold both families, the one she married into and the one she left behind, before the weight became too much. I realized in that moment that I had to protect my wife, just like how Raj protected Charmaine by moving her away from the drama and bad mind people.

The next day I wanted to speak to my old lady, and I had an off feeling about it, but I was sure I had to stand up. I waited until the children were settled. I saw Anil, Percy, and Amara go through the gate with their schoolbags. I noticed Devi went to the kitchen to put away the breakfast we had.

I stepped onto the veranda. Ma was there folding laundry on the rocking chair, slow and deliberate, her eye sharp as ever.

"Mama," I began, careful but firm, "Devi been here more than a year now. She has only seen her family three times. Is not cross the world them live, is just a bus ride away. She give this house everything, Ba, the children, you. But she miss her people. I want to take her to Papine for this weekend, let her see her family."

Her hands stilled on the cloth. She did not look up. "And who going mind this house while unu galivant off. Your father need watching, the children need steady hands. You is the man of this house now. Your wife belong here."

I clenched my jaw. "I not leaving the house empty. I was thinking to ask Charmaine and Raj to come by, just for a day. She can help. He can manage Ba."

My mother's head snapped up so fast her kerchief shifted. "No. That girl don't need to step foot in here. Not with her ways."

"Then my sisters," I pressed. "They can come, they would want to help."

Her bangles clattered as she slammed the cloth onto the table. "No. Them married out, they don't belong here no more. This is your house now. Your wife chose this family and she must stay where she vow to stay. Her duty here, not running back and forth like some young girl."

Her words cut deep, sharp as the iron she used to press my school uniform. For a moment I almost bent under it. But then I thought of Devi, sitting alone in the moonlight, her eyes turned to the hills she had not seen in too long.

I straightened. "Mama, duty don't mean prison. She not a servant. She is my wife, and she is still someone's daughter, someone's sister. If this house is going to survive, it is because of her. So do not tell me she cannot go see her own people."

Her eyes blazed, but I did not back down. For once, I stood in the silence she left, knowing the fight was far from over but also knowing Devi was worth every word.

A sound behind me made me turn. Devi stood in the doorway, her hands damp from washing, eyes wide, lips pressed tight. She had heard every word. For a moment her gaze flicked between me and Mama, one face fierce, the other defiant.

Her voice was quiet but steady. "I did not ask for quarrel. I only miss them. But if it shameful for me to want to see my family more often, then maybe I ask too much."

The silence that followed cut sharper than Mama's anger.

I crossed the room and took her hand, holding it firm in mine.

“No, Devi. You ask nothing wrong. And I not asking permission anymore. We going to Papine.”

My mother’s face tightened, her eyes like fire, but I did not let go of my wife’s hand. For once, I chose her in front of everyone, and I felt her grip steady against mine.

After the quarrel, I knew my mother was not going to make this easy. She had shut the door on Charmaine, refused to let Raj stand in, and turned her nose at my sisters as though their marriages erased them from our blood. But if Devi and I were going to spend a few days in Papine, I needed someone I could trust to keep an eye on Ba and the children.

The words rang in my ears, “This is your house now. Your wife belongs here.” But I was not about to let her rule Devi’s life like a chain.

That night, after Mama had gone to bed and the house quieted, I slipped onto the veranda. My nephew, sharp as ever, sat with a slate on his lap.

“You going Papine?” he asked, his grin wide.

I lowered my voice. “If I can find a way to reach your mom and aunty.”

He tapped his chalk. "I can run a note to Mommy or get a call to her. Nobody will know."

I scribbled a letter under the lamplight, nothing long, just a few words to my sisters: Come by the house. I need your help with Ba.

The boy tucked it into his pocket, eager to help me with any errand. I knew by morning he would find a way to slip it out past Mama's watchful eyes, running through Kingston lanes like a messenger of old.

As I sat there in the night breeze, I thought of my sisters. Riya with her ability to love and care, Kamala with her sternness. If they came, even for two days, the burden would be so much lighter. Shanti would not be able to handle the house alone, and Anil was still a minor. Mama might rage, but she could not deny her daughters.

For Devi's sake I was willing to risk any fury. Better that than let her wither in silence, missing her own people while carrying so much weight.

Within three days my sisters arrived. I heard their voices before I saw them, Kamala's firm tone and Riya's voice of love and gentle calm. They swept into the yard together, skirts rustling, arms full of fruits and sweets from country.

Riya's pregnant belly looked like she was ready to pop any day now.

Mama came out. "Who send for you?"

I stepped forward before they could answer. "I did. I am the man of the house now. Ba needs eyes on him while I head to Papine for a few days with Devi. Who better than his own daughters?"

"They married out. Their duty is to their husband house, not mine. Riya's father in law is ill too."

My sisters never flinched. "We may be married Ma, but we still your children. We still the daughters of unu. You think we would not come?"

Shanti came out the front room. She linked her arm through Devi's, who stood at the doorway. "And do not forget, Devi need her family too. She has to see her own people, just like how Riya and Kamala come to see us when they can."

The yard fell silent. Even the children watched, sensing the storm.

My mother's lips pressed thin, her face tight with fury. She opened her mouth, but Ba coughed from his chair, his hand twitching toward his girls. His words came out slurred and broken, but clear enough. “Let… them… stay.”

That was all it took.

Mama turned away sharply, muttering under her own breath, but she did not send them out. My sisters set their baskets down, moving about the house like they never left, laughing with the children, steadying Ba with quiet hands.

Devi’s eyes shone, a mix of relief and gratitude, though she said nothing.

That night, as the house settled, I sat on the front veranda watching my sisters fuss over our father and the children. I knew Riya missed Percy and Amara every day, but the schools here were far better for them. I knew eventually they would go back to country with her, but for now, watching her with them reminded me of how she took care of me when I was a child.

For the first time in months, the weight on Devi’s shoulders seemed lighter. She would have her days in Papine completely free, not as an escape, but as a daughter and a sister returning home.

And I knew, no matter how much Mama tried to hold her here, Devi had already carved her place in this house, not by obedience but by love.

CHAPTER 15: FIRST A DAUGHTER. ALWAYS A SISTER

The road to Papine wound through green hills, dust rising behind the cart wheels as we drew closer. Devi sat behind me, her eyes bright, her hands clasped tight in her lap. She had not seen her family in months. Even though they were just a short bus ride away, duty according to my mother had kept her back. I knew the weight of longing had pressed on her. Now with each turn, I could feel her whole body lean forward, as if she might jump out before the bus even stopped.

When we reached the yard, children burst out of the doorway, barefoot, shouting her name. Her sisters ran after them, skirts flying, their laughter rising above the goats bleating at the edge of the yard. Devi was swept up before I could even climb down, her mother pressing her face against hers, her father's arms around them both. It was chaos, loud, messy, joyful chaos, and it was beautiful.

Her father clapped me on the back, pulling me into the swirl. "Boy yuh finally bring back she to we. We thought Franklin

Town lock her away forever." His laugh was booming, his eyes kind.

The house was filled with more life than I had seen in months. Pots clanged, laughter spilled out, voices overlapped, and the smell of fresh roti and fish filled the air. Her sisters teased her mercilessly. "Look at you now, a wife with gold bangles? Yuh forget we Dev?" Her brothers argued over who missed her the most.

I sat back, struck by the difference. In Franklin Town the air was heavy with duty, my mother's sharp tongue and Ba's silence weighing down the rooms. Here in Papine, life burst out of every corner, messy and loud and joyful. Nobody asked about duty. Nobody whispered about respectability. They simply loved her, because she was theirs.

Food appeared in waves, dhal, callaloo, rice, roti hot off the tawa, mutton, fried fish. Her father poured me a drink, clapping me on the back and asking me if I was taking care of his daughter. If I said no, I knew they would all come back to Franklin Town to carry her away. Their laughs shook the room, and I laughed with them, though a part of me knew they were serious.

Devi moved among them glowing, her hands full of plates, her sari tugged by children, her laughter ringing free. She looked younger here, lighter, as if she shed the weight of her in laws' house the moment she stepped off the bus.

Later, when the sun dipped low, I found her on the veranda with her mother. They sat close, heads bent together, speaking a mix of Hindi, Bhojpuri, and patois. Her mother's hand stroked her hair like she was still a girl. Devi's face shone with tears, but her smile never faltered.

When I approached, her mother looked at me, eyes sharp but kind. "You have a good wife. Don't let she heart dry out. Remember before she was your wife, she was my daughter."

Those words sank deep. For all the love Devi gave to my family, to my community, she was tethered here, to this yard, to these people. And I knew then, part of her would always belong here, to Papine.

As night fell, music drifted from the yard, cousins beating drums, the younger ones singing. Devi stood in the middle, her sisters circling her, her brothers playing along. She danced with them, free and radiant, no longer a daughter in law under my mother's eyes, no longer second mother. Here she was what she had always been, a daughter, a sister, the heart of this house.

I watched from the edge, proud and humbled. For once, I was not the center of her world. Papine had claimed her back, if only for a weekend.

We slept in Barry's room, the room warm with the feeling of joy and laughter. I woke once in the night to see her sitting up, gazing out through the shutters at the hills. Her face was calm, but her eyes shimmered with longing.

By morning the house was loud again, children racing, her mother stirring pots of porridge. Devi helped in the kitchen, her hands moving with ease, her old rhythm returning as if she never left. She moved between stove and table like water flowing, laughing at her sisters' chatter, humming as she kneaded dough.

Her father noticed and shook his head, chuckling. "See how she belong here still? The restaurant miss her. Unu thief her way too soon."

Devi smiled, though her eyes fell for just a second. She missed it, the restaurant, the work, the steady clatter of pots and the chatter of customers. She was a stay at home wife now in Franklin Town, her days bound to another family. But here, in Papine, her hands remembered freedom.

After lunch, dhal, rice, and choka served in a noisy, joyful crowd, it was time to go. Her sisters clung to her, her brothers shouted promises to visit, her mother pressed food into her hands. Her father stood tall, his arm around her shoulders, as if to hold her just a moment longer.

Devi smiled and waved, but when the bus arrived, her tears spilled quietly. She did not weep loud, not Devi. She sat beside me with her back straight, her hands trembling in mine, her eyes fixed on the hills until they were swallowed by distance.

I knew she loved me, loved life with me. But I also knew that part of her heart would always ache for this, for her family, for the restaurant, for her home, the people that still called her daughter and sister first, before anyone's wife.

It struck me then, marriage had given her a new name, a new house, new duties. But it had taken something too. In Franklin Town she was a wife, an in law, a second mother. Here in Papine, she was herself, the heart of a house that welcomed her without condition.

I realized I had asked her to give up more than I ever had. I still had my brothers, my sisters, my father in his chair, my mother fierce in her way. She had left hers behind. She smiled at our house, yes, but part of her heart stayed in the hills, in the restaurant she no longer worked, in the laughter of her brothers and sisters.

As the hills disappeared behind us, I promised myself I would never let her spirit dry out under the weight of duty. Because before she was my wife, she was a daughter and a sister. And if I wanted her love to last, I would have to honor every part of who she was, not just the parts that belonged to me.

CHAPTER 16 WHEN FATHERS FALTER

The joy of Papine clung to us on the road back, but as soon as we stepped into Franklin Town, the air grew heavier. The house was quieter, darker. Ba was worse, his cough deeper, his walk slower, his words tangled almost beyond understanding. Ma hovered sharp as ever, but fear hid behind her eyes.

Riya had to head back to country, ready to give birth any day now. Percy and Amara went with her for a few days, eager to be there for the baby's arrival. The house felt empty without my two favorite people.

Kamala returned to her family, not wanting to miss Lilly's first steps and needing to attend to her ailing mother-in-law. Shanti was glowing with news of her engagement to a tall, lanky man from West Kingston, and Ma was pleased because his last name traced miles back to the Ganges.

Anil was finding his own stride, testing his charm in every lane of Kingston. The shop girls and market women knew his smile too well. Mama scolded him often, but Anil only grinned.

For me, the weight pressed down. Every task, every voice, every problem found its way to me. I was the man of the house now. I had never asked for it, but there it was. With Raj and Charmaine keeping their distance, it fell to me to steady the family. They came by now and then. He sat quiet, she smiled warm, Baby Jo darting all over the yard. They never stayed long. The space between them and us was as heavy as Ba's silence.

Later that week, I noticed something in Devi. She carried on with her duties, but sometimes I caught her wincing, her hand pressed against her stomach. She brushed it off as bellyache, but the shadow in her eyes told me it was more. I wondered if it was because she missed home, her family, being more than just a wife. Yet she cooked, cleaned, and tended Ba as if nothing had changed.

The house felt like a boat leaning under too many tides. Ba sinking, Mama stubborn, Shanti preparing to leave, Anil drifting, Raj visiting like a stranger. Through it all, Devi and I tried to hold the center, though I could feel it slipping. For the first time in my life, I truly understood what it meant to carry the weight of a family.

A few weeks later, the day began before the sun cleared the breadfruit tree. Devi was already in the kitchen, firewood snapping, the smell of saltfish and breadfruit drifting through the house. She moved carefully, pausing now and then to press her hand against her belly, but still making sure Ba's tea was hot, the porridge sweet enough, and Mama's voice answered with her calm, "Yes, Ma."

I rose to find Ba struggling to sit upright in his chair. His stroke had weakened him further, his words twisted, his steps dragging. I helped him outside to catch the breeze, his hand heavy on my shoulder. Where once he had led us, now I was leading him, and I felt the shift heavy in my chest.

The house bustled around me. Shanti fluttered, half distracted with talk of her engagement. Aunties whispered, Mama frowned at costs, cousins gossiped about saris. Anil breezed in and out, shirt half open, hair slicked, boasting about girls in class and in the market. I shook my head at him but smiled a little. He was still a boy pretending at manhood, while responsibility pressed harder on me each day.

By evening, after returning from work, I saw Devi at the pipe, sleeves wet, little cousins splashing more than helping. Her laugh rang out, but I noticed the strain in her eyes when she thought no one was watching. She missed her freedom, and I could sense her body tiring.

Shanti was on the veranda feeding Ba, spoon by spoon, with Ma hovering close. Later, after dishes were washed and children tucked in, I sat on the veranda with Ba at my side, his silence broken only by his labored breath. Devi brought me tea, her hand brushing mine, her eyes saying what words did not. This house leans on us now.

That was how our days went, one blurring into another. My father fading, Mama clinging to control, Shanti preparing to leave, Anil chasing laughter in the streets, Raj visiting when he could, Riya dropping in and sending letters when she could, and Kamala updating us on her life when she found the time. And Devi and I, side by side, carrying more weight than we ever expected.

The house still stood, but it leaned heavier on us with each passing day.

I began to notice the small things about Devi. At the pipe, she would pause, one hand pressed against her belly, her smile tight. In the kitchen, she leaned on the counter for a moment before lifting the heavy pots, her laughter spilling out but her body betraying its tiredness. At night, when the house was still, I sometimes found her curled on the cot, her hand resting on her stomach as if cradling something unseen.

One evening I asked, “Is it the food again?” She shook her head with a faint smile. “It comes and goes. Just little pain.”

My mother noticed too. She clucked her tongue, telling Devi she was working too hard or too soft. My father, quiet in his chair, only watched her, his weak eyes following her as if he saw what the rest of us would not say.

And me, I carried the unspoken thought in the back of my mind. Could it be more than a bellyache? Could it be that in the middle of all this heaviness, life was beginning again? I did not press her. Not yet. But I knew. Somewhere between the ache in her step and the softness of her smile, I knew.

The Message

Later that week, Devi wrote a note under the dim glow of the oil lamp. Her hand trembled as she folded the scrap of paper and tucked it into Shanti’s pocket.

“Bring my sister to Franklin Town. Quietly, I need her counsel. I think I may be carrying.”

Shanti left before dawn, giving the note to a messenger boy she trusted. By evening, her sister had the message in her hand.

Two days later, Devi's sister arrived on York Street, her skirt dusty from travel, her eyes anxious. She did not come with noise or crowd, only slipped through the gate, calling softly for her sister.

But my mother met her at the door.

"You turn back now," Mama snapped, blocking the way. "Devi have duties here. She married into this family. She cannot run back and forth to Papine every minute so."

The younger woman's face flushed hot with shame and anger. She tried to explain, her words tripping over themselves. "It is not bellyache, Ma'am. She need me. I am her sister…"

But Mama's bangles clattered as she waved her off. "She busy. I will not have outsiders stirring up my house."

Hurt and furious, she turned on her heel and left. But she did not go home. She went straight to the restaurant, fire in her chest, straight to her eldest brother.

"She called for me," she told him, voice breaking. "She not well. She think she with child, and the mother turn me away from her door."

Barry's jaw set. He was not a man of many words, but when he rose, the room shifted. "Then I go myself. Nobody turn family away when she call."

Back in Franklin Town, Devi sat on the veranda steps, her hands pressed to her stomach, waiting. She did not know if her sister would return, or if the message had been lost. But she prayed that soon, someone from Papine would walk through the gate and stand beside her.

The yard was quiet that morning, my father dozing in his chair, the children playing marbles under the steps. Then came the sound of footsteps, steady and unhurried but heavy with purpose.

When I looked up, there he was—Barrington, the same brother I bowled out nearly two years ago. He stood tall and broad, his face stern. He did not wait to be invited in. He walked straight through the gate, his eyes sweeping the yard until they found my mother by the doorway.

"Ma," he said, voice low but firm. "We need to talk."

Mama straightened, her bangles clattering as she crossed her arms. “This is my yard. Speak.”

“My sister called for help,” he said. “She send for her own blood. And you turn her away? She think she carrying child, and you shame her by refusing her sister?”

Mama’s nostrils flared. “She married into this family. She is mine to guide now. If she weak, she must lean here, not run back home for every ache.”

“She nuh weak,” he shot back. “She strong. Stronger than anyone me know. But just because she strong don’t mean she don’t need her people. Before she was your daughter-in-law, she was our daughter, our sister. That nuh change because she wear ring.”

The yard was still. Even the children stopped their game to stare. Devi stood frozen in the doorway, her eyes wide, one hand pressed to her stomach.

I stepped forward, unsure, because I had not even known Devi’s sister had come. What else had I missed?

I placed myself between them. “He is right, Mama. Devi give everything to this house. But she need support now, not weight. If her family want to visit her and stand by her, why chase them off?”

Mama's mouth pressed thin. For a long moment I thought she would erupt, send him away, send all of us away if she could. But Ba coughed from his chair, his broken voice cutting through the tension. "Let them stay."

Mama turned her face aside, silent. She did not agree. But she could not send him out either.

Barry walked past me then, into the house, straight to his sister's side. He placed a hand on her shoulder, steady and protective. "We here now," he murmured.

Devi finally let the tears fall—not loud, but enough to show the relief that had been buried inside her. And in that moment, Franklin Town felt less like a cage. For the first time, her two families stood in the same yard, and Devi was not alone anymore.

By late afternoon, the gate creaked again. This time it was Devi's sister, the one Mama had turned away days before. But she did not come timid or apologetic. She came with Barry at her side, his presence like a shield.

Mama stiffened when she saw them, but she said nothing. The eldest brother's warning had been enough. His silent authority filled the yard, and Mama, though fuming, did not dare send the girl off again.

Inside the house, Devi's sister ran straight to her, taking her hands. "I should have never left without you," she whispered, her eyes shining. "I come back as soon as I could."

Devi tried to smile, but her lips trembled. "I thought… maybe I carrying." Her hand pressed against her. "I don't know for sure, but something feel different."

Her sister pulled her into an embrace, rocking her gently the way their mother would have. "You are not alone. If it true, it is a blessing."

They sat together for hours in private, talking about cravings and missed cycles, about the changes only sisters could speak of. Devi admitted her fear, not of being a mother, but of facing it under Mama's stern gaze, with Ba fading and the house leaning so heavy on her.

Barry lingered outside the doorway, his arms crossed, his eyes watchful. He did not intrude, but his silence spoke louder than words. This time she would have her family by her side.

For the first time in months, Devi seemed to breathe easier. She was not just a wife, or a daughter-in-law carrying duties. She was a sister again, a daughter again, wrapped in the comfort of people who knew her before York Street claimed her.

After all the noise and everyone had left, the house settled. For once the world was quiet enough for just the two of us.

Devi sat beside me on the bed, her hair loose, her face pale from the long day. She took my hand and placed it gently on her belly.
"I been holding this too long," she whispered. "I think… no, I know. I am carrying."

Her words hit me harder than any factory shift. My heart pounded, my breath caught, and for a moment I could not find my voice. I just stared at her, her eyes glistening but steady.
"You sure?" I asked at last, though I already knew from the way her body had been speaking before her lips did.

She nodded, pressing my hand firmer against her. "I feel it. And my sister feel it too. I did not want to tell you until I was certain. But I cannot hide it no more."

I pulled her close, wrapping my arms around her. For weeks I had watched her strain under Mama's demands, bend over Papa's chair, hush the children while hiding her own pain. And now, knowing she carried life inside her, our life, I felt both joy and fear rising together.
"Devi," I murmured against her hair, "this house already lean heavy on you. But you will not carry this alone. Not this time."

She smiled faintly, relief softening her face. "I prayed you would say that."

And as the night wrapped around us, I realized the weight of the house had shifted again, but this time it was not only burden. It was promise.

The next morning Devi's sister slipped back into the yard to check on her. After a few minutes together inside, I heard their laughter, low and secretive, a kind of relief spilling out between them. Her sister hugged her, eyes shining. By midday the younger cousins already guessed something was different. Children always noticed before adults, and the word baby danced on their tongues in giggles.

Papa's Joy

Papa was the first elder to know. Devi knelt beside him with a bowl of porridge, and instead of scolding her for being too slow, Mama noticed his hand shaking as he reached to touch her belly. His broken words came out rough, but clear enough.

"Grand child."

The whole room stilled. Papa's eyes were wet, and for the first time in months his smile broke through the weakness.

Mama's Reaction

But Mama's face glowed with pride. She did not say it or clap her hands. She crossed her arms, her voice sharp as cut cane.

"Another mouth to feed. More work for this house. And she already soft with bellyaches. Who going tend Papa when she too weak? Who going cook when she too tired?"

Her words cut, but no one answered her. Even the children fell silent.

The Ripple

By evening the news had spread across Franklin Town. Aunties passed it between them with raised brows, uncles muttered that it was time already, and neighbors leaned over the fence to whisper. Some smiled wide and offered blessings, others looked at Mama to see how she would spin it.

Through it all, Devi kept her head high, though I could see her hand drifting to her stomach, protective and tender.

The months passed quickly, and the weight on Devi's shoulders began to change. No longer just the burden of Franklin Town, she now carried something new, something alive. Her steps slowed, yes, but her smile widened. The children adored her belly, pressing their ears against it, giggling at the faint kicks. Even Papa, in his weakened state, would reach for her hand with a soft smile whenever she entered the room, as if her glow eased his pain.

Every few weeks she went back to Papine, her brothers and sisters fussing over her, her mother pressing food into her hands, her father blessing her belly. Those visits reminded her of who she was before Franklin Town claimed her, and they gave her the strength to keep going.

One cool morning she traveled with Amara, her niece by marriage, to the University Hospital of the West Indies in Mona. The walls were tall and white, the halls echoing with footsteps, the smell of antiseptic sharp. A young Indian doctor greeted them kindly, pressing a stethoscope to her belly and nodding at the steady heartbeat within.

"Strong child," he said with a smile. "Everything progressing well."

Devi squeezed Amara's hand, relief softening her face. For once she was being tended to, not tending to others.

Almost Christmas

By December the house smelled of sorrel and fresh pine sprigs, and carol singers passed the lanes at night. The household, heavy with worry most of the year, felt a spark of joy in the air. Even Mama, though still sharp, could not hide the pride that her son and Devi were about to bring new life into the family.

Devi, heavy with child, spent most of her days on the veranda, humming softly while the little ones played at her feet. She spoke often of her mother's Christmas puddings in Papine, her father's laughter, her brothers' games, her sisters' chatter. "I want my child to know both homes," she whispered to me one night.

On a December night, the Franklin Town house was filled with both fear and anticipation. Devi's labor came strong and fast, the women bustling around her, the midwife whispering prayers between instructions. Her cries filled the air, then finally, the sharp, piercing wail of new life: a baby girl, small but fierce, her tiny fists already curled tight.

The family gathered, awestruck. Devi, exhausted but radiant, cradled her daughter, pressing kisses to her damp forehead. I stood beside them, overwhelmed by joy and disbelief, knowing our world had shifted forever.

But across the house, in his chair on the veranda, Papa grew weaker. The stroke had already robbed him of much, and the long months had worn him thin. That same night, as his granddaughter cried for the first time, Papa drew in one last rattled breath. His pipe slipped from his fingers, and his body slumped.

Shanti found him first, rushing to his side, her own cry tearing through the house. Mama's wails followed, sharp and broken, as the family scrambled around him.

Two Currents in One House

One side of the house filled with life, the other with death. Devi clutched our daughter tighter as she heard the commotion, her eyes wet with both joy and dread. I moved between rooms, torn — one hand touching the tiny softness of new life, the other gripping the still shoulder of the man who had raised me.

Neighbors poured in as the word spread. "Baby born. Papa gone." They shook their heads in awe and sorrow, whispering of the circle of life, of how the ancestors sometimes step aside to make space for the new.

By dawn, the house was changed forever. A little girl had entered the world, carrying our hope, while Papa had left it, carrying his silence. Mama sat between the two rooms, her face streaked with tears, whispering prayers to both gods and ancestors. Devi, pale but glowing, pressed our daughter into my arms. "She will know him," she whispered. "Even if she never remember his voice, she will know him."

And I understood then. The weight of the house had shifted again, heavier than ever, yet lightened by the tiny cry of the child who would carry us into tomorrow.

The Day of Mourning

The day of the funeral dawned gray, as if the sky itself carried the heaviness we felt. Franklin Town was hushed, neighbors moved slowly, dressed in black and white, their faces solemn. The house filled with relatives from near and far, some we had not seen since Kamala's wedding, others arriving unannounced, drawn by the news that the patriarch of our family had gone.

Papa's body lay in the front room, draped in white, the air heavy with incense and the low murmur of prayers. Mama sat near him, her eyes swollen from weeping, her bangles muted against her lap. Devi moved quietly, carrying water, arranging food, whispering comfort to those who came to pay respects, even though her own body still ached from childbirth.

It seemed like the entire Indian community showed up at May Pen Cemetery that Saturday. At the churchyard, the tassa drums were silent, replaced by the solemn toll of bells. Men carried Papa's coffin on their shoulders, the weight of it pressing into all of us. I walked beside them, my daughter in my arms, her small face pressed against my chest.

The preacher spoke of life's circle, one man leaving, another generation beginning. Though his words were meant for comfort, they felt like a command. The spade clinked against stone as the earth covered him, each thud final and echoing. Mama wept openly, her body shaking. Riya held on to her children, Kamala held on to Lilly, Shanti clung to me, Anil stood stiff but pale, and Raj Jr. lingered at the edge with Charmaine, his silence heavy.

When the crowd thinned, eyes began to turn toward me. Uncles clasped my shoulder harder than usual, cousins nodded in recognition. “You the man of the house now,” they said. “Papa gone, but you must lead.”

The words settled on me like stone. I looked down at my daughter, so small in my arms, and then at Devi, standing steady despite her exhaustion. My heart swelled with fear and pride at once.

That night, back in Franklin Town, the house felt emptier than ever. Papa’s chair sat vacant on the veranda, his pipe resting where he had left it. Mama sat silently beside it, staring into the dark.

I stood in the doorway, my daughter cradled against me. I knew there would be no more leaning on Papa’s silence, no more waiting for him to nod approval or give counsel. The weight of this house was mine now — its duties, its quarrels, its survival.

And as I looked at Devi holding the lamp steady, our baby nestled in her arms, I realized I was no longer just a son or a brother. I was the father, the man of the family, and there was no turning back.

I sat on the veranda that night, my daughter asleep in my arms, and my thoughts drifted back to Mama. I remembered when I was a boy, before the years hardened her voice, when her laughter used to ring through the house. Back then she was softer, her eyes brighter, her hands busy but not bitter. She and Papa would share quiet looks, little smiles, as if the whole yard belonged to their love.

But something shifted. Years of holding the house alone, raising children without help, watching Papa's silence grow heavier, watching traditions slip away, it carved her into someone else. Duty had turned into armor. She clung to customs like they were the only thing keeping her upright. The warmth in her laugh was replaced by sharpness in her tongue.

As I watched Devi rocking our daughter later that night, I asked myself if this was the path for us too. Would time, hardship, and duty grind down her gentleness the way it did Mama's? Would the weight of this house and the burden of family turn her joy into steel?

The thought terrified me. Because I loved Devi not just for her strength, but for her laughter, her kindness, the way she made even Papa's silence lighter. I couldn't bear the idea of her losing that.

I whispered a promise to myself, one I didn't dare speak aloud: I would not let duty swallow us whole. I would not let Devi's love dry out the way Mama's did. The house leaned on us now, yes, but we would carry it together, not alone.

Because if Mama's life was a warning, then mine had to be different. For Devi, for our daughter, for me.

CHAPTER 17. THE HOUSE THAT HELD US

The house in Franklin Town leaned heavier than ever, but it did not fall. My daughter's cry filled the same rooms where Papa's silence once sat. Life and death had crossed paths under this roof, and I now carried both.

Everywhere I turned, I could see the change. Riya was happily married and preparing Percy, Amara, and little Sheva for the next steps in their lives. Kam had Lilly and was now expecting another bundle anytime soon. Shanti was preparing for her own marriage, Anil was chasing laughter down Kingston's streets, and Raj lived quietly with Charmaine, visiting sparingly. My sisters wrote letters from their husbands' houses. The family had stretched, broken, mended, and stretched again.

But here, at the center, Devi and I remained. Her laughter was steady, her hands strong, her eyes carrying both Papine and Franklin Town inside them. She had given this family a daughter, but she had also given it something more: hope, renewal, a reason to keep moving.

I thought often of Papa, of the man who came to Jamaica with dreams of going home and never made it back. I thought of Mama, her love hardened into duty, her sharp words hiding the ache of years. And I wondered if that would one day be us.

But then I would look at Devi, rocking our baby, Jaine, on the veranda, her hair falling loose as she hummed a Bhojpuri tune, and I knew I could choose differently. We could honor the roots without letting them chain us. We could build something new, even here in this island soil.

As New Year bells rang across Kingston, and the breeze carried both church hymns and tassa drums through the lanes, I felt the weight of everything we had lost and everything we had gained.

The house was smaller now without Papa, without my sisters, without the noise of the old days. But it was still alive. And as I watched my daughter curl into Devi's arms, her tiny breath steady against her chest, I realized the house would live on.

Because in the end, that is what family does. It bends, it breaks, it remakes itself. It remembers the dead, and it holds the living.

And as long as I had Devi, as long as I had the child we made together, the house would still stand.

After Papa died, it was Devi who became the true pillar of Franklin Town. She was the one who steadied the house when grief threatened to split it open, who cooked when Mama could not rise, who kept the children clothed and fed when silence pressed heavy. People began to say it out loud now: "Second mother, backbone of the house."

Through her hands, the family did not scatter entirely. Even when others pulled away, she held the center.

One by one, my brothers and sisters went their own way. Kamala settled deeper into her husband's home, Shanti built her own family, Raj stayed with Charmaine, far enough that his visits became rare. Anil was the only one who lingered, restless yet tethered, too loyal to leave Mama alone.

And me, though part of me longed to follow, to build a life just for Devi and the children, I stayed. For the house was not done with us yet, and I had the sense that our story in Franklin Town was only beginning another chapter.

The Man of the House

Staying meant sacrifice. There were days I wanted to take Devi and run, give her a house of her own where Mama's sharp tongue could not weigh her down. But duty kept me rooted. Mama had lost her husband, and though she grew harder with age, she was still my mother. She depended on us now, and it fell on me to make sure she was never abandoned.

So the years stacked one on the other. Devi bore me four children, each one bright, each one carrying her laughter and strength. They grew up under that same roof, where Mama watched over them with stern but loving eyes, and Papa's empty chair sat as memory.

Now, when I look back, I see the choice I made. I stayed when others left. I stayed for Mama, for duty, for the promise I could not break. Sometimes I wonder what life might have been if I had left, if I had chosen freedom for Devi and me. But then I see her with our children, her arms steady, her heart unshaken, and I know the truth.

It was Devi who carried us all, through Papa's silence, through Mama's hardness, through the shifting of generations. She was the backbone, not me. I only held on because she held me up.

And though the house leaned, it never fell.

EPILOGUE.

Years have passed now. My children are grown, with children of their own tugging at their skirts and trousers. The noise of little feet still fills the veranda, though my hair has silvered and my hands move slower than they once did.

The house in Franklin Town is not what it was in my youth. The walls lean, the paint has faded, the mango tree in the yard grows wilder each year. But it still stands. Just as I still stand.

Mama is gone now, her sharp voice finally softened by silence. I think of her often, how duty shaped her, how love hardened into control. I spent years fearing Devi would become the same, but she never did. Devi carried weight without letting it break her. She was the laughter when the house fell quiet, the oil that kept the gears moving, the hand steady enough to hold us all. She was, and remains, the backbone.

When my grandchildren sit at my feet, asking for stories, I tell them about Papa who came from India but never went back, about Mama who held the house together through fire and storm, about my brothers and sisters who scattered across the island. But most of all, I tell them about Devi, the girl from Papine who walked into Franklin Town and gave it new life.

And when the night grows still, I look at her across the yard, her sari brushing the floor as she bends to gather a grandchild, her hair streaked with silver, her smile still soft. I know then that no matter how much has passed, no matter how much has been lost, we built something lasting here.

The house remembers. And through our children, our grandchildren, and the love that carried us through, the house will stand long after I am gone. But houses do not only hold the past. They wait for the future. Already, I see it in the bright eyes of those who run barefoot across the veranda, asking questions I cannot yet answer. Their story is still unwritten. And one day, they will tell it.

For Mama and Papa, the house still stands because of you.

AFTERWORD

This story was inspired by the lives of my grandparents. It is not their story exactly, but the heart of it — the struggles, the sacrifices, the laughter, and the love — belongs to them.

My grandmother was the true backbone of our family. She carried more than her share, holding everyone together with strength that seemed endless. My grandfather, in contrast, was the jokester, always quick with a laugh, always lightening the weight of the world with humor.

He once told me something I've never forgotten: "If she dies first, I could live many years without her. But if I die first, she could only last a year without me." And that is exactly how it happened. His words were not just a joke, but a truth about how deeply they belonged to each other.

I am blessed to have known them, to have listened to their stories, and to carry their memories forward. This book is my way of honoring them, their courage, their devotion, and the lessons they left behind about love, family, and resilience.

To my grandparents: thank you for the gift of your lives. May this story keep your spirit alive for generations to come.

ACKNOWLEDGMENTS

Thank you to my Uncle Sunil. You taught me how to read, and with that, you gave me the world. There would be no book without you.

Thank you to my Aunty Sandra. You laid the path so I could choose my own. Always Pumpkin.

Thank you to my Aunty Marie Every time you cook, it reminds me of Mama. The flavors and love you put into it—make me feel like a piece of her is still here.

Thank you Kayla. Our grandmothers were sisters, and now so are we. They were the roots, now we bloom.

Thank you Dania. You always manage to seek out the good in me even when I stumble, and remind me of the right path in every wrong.

Thank you Shannan. Your presence was shelter, your friendship warmth in every season. Your support and loyalty mean the world to me, and I am truly grateful to have you in my life.

Thank you Donnia and Karella. Growing up near you both at different times of my life shaped me in so many ways, and your influence has been a blessing in my life.

Thank you to Raquel Jones. A friend like breeze through mango trees, gentle, sure, and always near. We go together like roti and curry goat.

Thank you to Cry. You taught me how to love and comfort every type of soul. Everyone needs a friend like you.

Thank you, Lori. You taught me how to live outside the box and to never stop talking. Talking led to writing, and now I'm here and you're coming with me.

Thank you Aunty Margaret. You never let me be without a grandmother's love, not once. Your energy is the comfort I still need in this thing we call life.

Thank you Ling, for being the first person to look at my manuscript, bit by bit. Your enthusiasm and love stick with me and are part of my motivation. Those random facetimes and checkups you did for me did not go unnoticed.

Thank you Monet, for your endless support and kindness. I appreciate every ounce of courage you gave me along the way. "When is the book coming out?" kept me going.

Thank you Roshida. You came into my life when I was still finding myself, and your spirit and encouragement helped me on that path. You have already made such a meaningful impact in my life, and we have so much more to go.

Thank you, Aunty Joan, for never leaving Mama's side, through the good and the bad. Your granddaughters will always have an Aunty in me.

Thank you to Jeffery James Sr. Our conversations stay in my heart and my mind forever. Thank you for listening, for sharing, and for seeing me. Love always, Poca.

Thank you to my parents, for buying me every book I ever wanted. I love you.

ABOUT THE AUTHOR

Ashley Prendergast was born in the Bronx, New York, to Natalie and Clifford, new immigrants building a life in a new land. At just four months old, she was taken to Jamaica by her grandparents, where she spent the early years of her life surrounded by the warmth of island culture. Her childhood unfolded between two worlds: the vibrant pulse of the Bronx and the deep-rooted traditions of Jamaica. This unique blend shaped her voice and perspective.

She returned to the Bronx to complete high school at St. Thomas Aquinas, an all-girls Catholic school, before heading south to Florida International University, where she earned her degree in Psychology. Today, Ashley works in Human Resources and is the proud mother of a loving twelve-year-old future soccer star who keeps her grounded and inspired.

Ashley's love for reading began early, thanks to her Uncle Sunil, who placed her first chapter book in her hands. From bookstore runs with her father and countless library trips with her mother, stories became her sanctuary. As she grew older, her curiosity led her deeper into the history of her Indian heritage and the indentured journey of her ancestors in Jamaica, stories she now honors through her writing.

She continues to live between her two loves, Jamaica and New York, carrying generations of history in her heart and a pen always within reach.

About the Author

www.ingramcontent.com/pod-product-compliance
Lightning Source LLC
Chambersburg PA
CBHW070539310726
48982CB00010B/1412/J

* 9 7 9 8 2 1 8 7 9 0 0 0 4 *